Deadlines and D**kheads

'I thought it was brilliantly funny. It's dark, mischievous, generous and contains some of the best comic writing I've read in years.'
Tommy Tiernan

'Mary McNice is priceless. I giggled and cringed along with her on her mad workday and even madder night ... she is a fabulous antidote to the countless milky watery eejits in books. Anne Gildea has created a brilliant character with a big heart full of mad contradictions and witty bravado. I was rooting for her scatty but lovable self from start to finish.'
Maeve Higgins, *Naked Camera*

'MaryMcNice is hilarious. Anne Gildea has created a kooky character with balls of steel – a true original.'
Quentin Fottrell, *The Sunday Tribune*

'Gildea has fashioned an uproarious, page-turning, razor-sharp exposé of Dublin's media whores and the shamelessly shallow world they mix in. In Mary McNice she has created a flawlessly flawed character to laugh at, laugh with and root for all the way, despite her blinkered self-delusion, questionable morals and bad hair moments.'
Brian Finnegan, *Gay Community News*

DEADLINES
AND
D**KHEADS

Anne Gildea

THE O'BRIEN PRESS
DUBLIN

First published 2006 by The O'Brien Press Ltd,
12 Terenure Road East, Rathgar, Dublin 6, Ireland.
Tel: +353 1 4923333; Fax: +353 1 4922777
E-mail: books@obrien.ie
Website: www.obrien.ie

ISBN-10: 0-86278-963-X
ISBN-13: 978-0-86278-963-3

British Library Cataloguing-in-Publication Data
Gildea, Anne
Deadlines and d**kheads
1.Women journalists - Ireland - Fiction 2.Self-actualization (Psychology) -
Fiction
I.Title II. Byrne, Eva
823.9'2[F]

1 2 3 4 5 6 7 8 9 10
06 07 08 09 10

Editing, typesetting, layout and design: The O'Brien Press Ltd
Illustrations: Eva Byrne
Author photograph: Marc O'Sullivan
Printing: Creative Print and Design, Wales

ACKNOWLEDGEMENTS

In the long preamble to this publication, many people, directly or obliquely, are implicated for thanks. To name check one is to name check all, so here goes.

Enormous thanks to Michael, Ide and all the team at The O'Brien Press, most especially to my editor, Mary Webb.

Thank you to my agent, John Saddler, and in the same breath, huge thanks, Aidan Hynes. Thank you to Brian Finnegan for encouragement at the very beginning.

Thanks with frills on to Quentin Fottrell for the speed boat 'n' champagne element of my 'research', and in this also big thanks to Lindsay Sedgwick, Tara Flynn, Conor Ferguson, and most especially to Alex Lyons for answering a query with the 'Come and Get It' chocolate idea, campaign and 'road to Damascus' moment. Deeply appreciative of that, Alex; you're a star.

Just-remembered-thanks to Nick Kelly for lending me that inspirational book many moons ago. Thank you for your spontaneous kindness.

Artistic-retreat-like thanks to all at the Tyrone Guthrie Centre, Annaghmakerrig. Spiritual thanks to Bill Darlison, Art Lester and the Stephen's Green gathering. Thank you, Janet Pierce, for problems halved.

Chums-o'er-the-miles thanks to Robin Molenaar, Larissa Kousnitsova, Antoinette Azzurro, Annmarie Gilkes, Shuna Snow and Patricia Dunne. Thank you for being there, and, all of you, for coming here this year. And also, deep Grecian appreciation to Constantina and Kyriaki Mpata for the company when I was writing on Folegandros and the welcome when I returned to Athens. Thank you so much.

Thank-you-for-you thanks also to Michelle Read, Sue Collins and Pom Boyd. Special thanks to Fergal Owens.

I-am-a-fortunate-sister thanks to my endlessly supportive, inspiring and brilliant brother, Kevin. Just-as-lucky-in-law thanks to Tracy, and in-awe thanks to new Alexander, and whirlwind Rosa. Thanks, Mum, for the endless supply of moisturiser – wrinkles have been visibly reduced.

Thank you, Lee Rennie-Brennan, for being the first to read and comment on an early draft, that is, first after my sister ...

Finally, sister, thank you, dear Una, for dropping everything whenever to read and reread the writing until you were cross-eyed with the process, brain-fried with McNiceness and on the verge of self-combustion at the sight of yet another rewritten sheaf. Sorry about all that. But big, big thanks.

For my incomparable sister, Una.

CHAPTER 1

He's six foot four, I don't need a tape measure to know, I can just tell by the way the handsome shovels of his hands have picked me up like I'm a soufflé and laid me on the smooth upholstery of his huge couch while he delights above me as if I were an Angelina Jolie soufflé, only better. 'I've waited so long for this,' I say in a voice like crème puffs. I know I've found him. HIM! Finally! He is absolutely all I've ever wanted in, oh feck, ever. Unfortunately he's completely indistinct. He's a blur. All I can make out is that he's big. Big, big, big, and strong like a bull. He snorts like a bull. 'Yes, yes, yes,' my heart says in Joycean abandon. 'Yes, let's get a mortgage. Together.'

I have to know who he is. 'What's your name? What's your name?' I'm asking him. We're at an altar. Coming, coming, oh God, it's coming into a close-up on his face, and he's about to say …

'It was my canoe, remember?'

Canoe? Where did that come from?

'*My* canoe, *my* canoe. Listen to yourself, you sound pathetic.'

Next door.

Voices.

Argument.

It is morning.

I am awakening.

Awake.

My name is Mary.

Mary McNice.

I am in my bed.

It is a double bed.

I am alone in it.

In my luxurious one-bedroom city centre apartment, 32m², bought five years ago (with my absentee brother – his investment, my lifesaver), a snip at €180,000, now worth a billion or something, management fees extra and subject to inflation, naturally.

'You bitch!'

Including Dimplex and Dumplux extractor fans, Electropox wall-mounted storage heaters, Plasticky Windows, Cardboardy Doors, Pretendy Wood Floors, Midget's Kitchen with mini cabinets, built-in space to hang a coat, and overall not enough room to swing a kitten. Oh, and party walls thin as a Tayto.

'You bastard.'

Mortgage 3.79% APR and rising.

'Bollocks.'

Oh, the buzz of having a variable rate.

'Cow.'

I hate my life. Correction: I hate my life compared to the horny Nirvana I just had in my sleep, in my head. It was real, it felt real, I want to feel it again and forever, I want, I want and I want …

'Oh, feck off.'

I want, I want, I want, as much as anybody wants in these wanty times.

'You feck off.'

I put the pillow over my head. There's a pair of yellowy-white, over-used, sticky, blobby, frankly disgusting wax earplugs in the dust on the floor under the bed, somewhere within reach, but I leave them. They're for Garda helicopters hovering endlessly overhead, alcohol-induced student behaviour, junky fisticuffs, cats at it in the local alley, and alarms yowling for hours for no one – typical neighbourhood night stuff. (The kind of stuff that never makes it into estate agents' 'most sought-after, convenient city centre location' hyperbole, natch.) Anyway, it seems a sin to block out morning noise; surely it's there to tell you it's time to get your arse in gear and get up?

I just want my dream back:

Manstrokebull bigbullman stroking my ohhh with his hoofhand ohbugger cockgone oohhh, nooooo ...

No. Give up.

My dream is gone forever. In the future there'll be some sort of zip-chip, and when you have a totally brilliant dream you'll be able simply to insert it in your ear when you wake and it will record in full detail the trace of brain activity involved in producing the pseudo-memories of the dream. Then you'll be able to relive your favourite dreams over and over. But not only that! Share them with your lover! And your lover can share their dreams with you! So finally we'll all be totally on the same beautiful page.

Something smashes next door. Jesus, I can't wait for the future.

It's 6:30am. The neighbours are having showers now. I hear the angry pad of naked feet on laminated wood floor, the extractor fan that goes on with the bathroom light, the gush of a hip-high pee (it's probably him), a fart (definitely), and the hum of the shower pump. They're not showering together. They often do.

They have sex in the shower, too. Saturday mornings, mainly, when they're not worried about high-flying it out the door. She likes to moan big time, 'give it to me baby, give it to me, baby' when he's giving it to her. Given the acoustics in the bathroom they might as well be doing it with six mics and mega amps on them, but that's probably all part of what gets her 'so horned up baby, oh yeah'.

I gather the to-do this morning is over a punctured canoe and responsibility theretofore. They're a sporty pair. They've the energy and enthusiasm of toddlers; as if all the world's another sporting activity waiting to be discovered. Every other weekend they're off with a pile of nautical fibre-glass yokes strapped to the roof of the SUV. The SUV is all part of the image.

'I'd say those fenders come in handy when there's a kangaroo on the M50,' I quipped to Mr O'Sport once, when they'd first moved in. He nodded and smiled but said nothing. He probably thought I was being sarky, but I was actually just trying to be flirty. There's no getting away from it – he's a hunk and a half, and who wouldn't want to be on chitty chatty terms with that?

I wanted to call after him and explain, 'you know, Roo-Bars they call them in Australia. For kangaroos. Gettit?' But I didn't, and he probably did get it because, let's face it, there wasn't really a lot to get, per se. And furthermore I bet they know Australia a lot better than I do. They both look like they've spent aeons there doing every water-based recreation Australia has ever thought of: surfing, body-surfing, wind-surfing, Aboriginal-bark surfing, para-gliding-with-a-tinnie-in-yer-mitt-sail surfing, or just plain skiing, diving, kayaking and nearly dying along the way at some stage, but laughing it off round the beach barbie later, and all the ladies in their near-nudie bikinis.

Am I jealous? Of course not! I've been to Australia myself. I went snorkelling near-shore once. Breege, my nervous friend-in-travel, stood on the jetty, screaming down at me to 'BEWARE OF THE SHARKS!!!' She thought she saw one and freaked me out of the water. It was only later in life I discovered that if you just give a shark a good thump on the nose he'll back off. But these are the kind of things you learn with time. Unless you're a successful, young, fit, sexy, modern Celtic graduate professional type like my neighbours. Those two were born knowing everything.

He's back in the bedroom, she's getting up, and they're starting at each other again, so it's a blessing that my mobile rings. They're reminded I'm here and hush up. Normally I wouldn't be well pleased with a 6:45am phone call, particularly from Miriam, my editor at *Midweek*.

'Mary, hi, I didn't wake you, did I?' she begins.

Midweek is the free Wednesday supplement with *The Irelander*, Ireland's first daily broadsheet to downsize to tabloid, or 'Berliner', as the likes of Miriam prefer to call it. 'They'll have to retitle it *The Irelandeen*,' my friend Declan joked at the time. 'The ABC1 mighty midget of Irish opinion-making marches on – left, right, left, right, right, right, down the middle of the road.'

'No, no,' I chirp, trying to sound like I've been out of bed for hours and instinctively feeling guilty that I haven't. *If you snooze you lose; you'll be asleep long enough in the long run*, my father always said. He's dead now himself. May he rest in peace; he's left it so that I never can.

'Oh, that's good. I just got a call from Chris Bell, he's flattened with the 'flu. Would you be free to cover an interview for him today?'

I get out of bed and stand up. *A clever trick is to stand when you're taking an important telephone call. You're asserting yourself, even if the person on the other end of the line doesn't realise it* – a remembered snatch of advice from the Etiquette Nun at school. I have to sound cool and collected because Miriam is offering me exactly what I have been hoping for.

Chris does most of the arts and entertainment interviewing for *Midweek*. He's just back from interviewing one of those X-treme 70s/80s US Super Groups in LA. You know the ones: skinny leather trousers, fat fly-away hair; every flap of flesh pierced; every drug shot, snorted, smoked, swallowed, sucked or just plain took. Every groupie groped and/or banged in a gang followed by marriage to various sets of tits, and a few tragic deaths thrown in for the craic along the way – the full Monty. I can't remember the name but that's the level Chris interviews at. I haven't a clue about rock, per se, but this could open up a whole plethora of other doors. Chris is a staffer, I'm not, and it's unusual that I would be asked to do an interview off the cuff like this. I'm not known as an interviewer. It's a great opportunity, a move-on from just ...

'Hello, hello, are you there?' Miriam asks.

'Yes, yes. And yes,' I answer, covering all questions.

'Yes, you'll do it?'

'Yes!' I declare confidently. Emphatically. Standing there, no knickers, in a ten-year-old 'Just say no' t-shirt – my sleep-alone bed wear.

'Great, well, that's great. You haven't heard who it is yet, but great,' she says. Is my enthusiasm breeding doubt?

'Yes?' I say, just to keep everything going along on the positive. It could be somebody huge, I could be catching a flight somewhere exotic in two minutes.

'It's Paddy Finn, Westbury Hotel, 4pm.'

Oh. 'Who? Sorry, didn't catch that?' Paddy Finn? The name rings a bell.

'Paddy Finn, stand-up comedian, star in the ascendant, etcetera and blah, blah. He opens for a run in Curate's Lane shortly. And he has the usual heap of other projects in the background: a DVD deal, some film and telly.'

Christ, I wonder why she's asking me? I wouldn't have considered myself the obvious first choice for something like that. And, as it turns out, I'm not.

'Seeing as Chris can't do it, and Paddy has limited availability, I thought it would be fun to send you to interview him,' she says, adding, 'and no one else was free. I thought you might put an "Attitude" spin on it, work it in as your next column?'

'Oh. Right. Great,' I enthuse, quietly crawling back under the duvet.

'Attitude' is the title of my *Midweek* column. Beside the bold heading, 'ATTITUDE', is a shot of me supposedly giving it loads. It was the photographer who suggested I cross my arms under my chest, tilt my head to one side, and wink. *And* wear the pink t-shirt with 'Just A Girlie' scrawled across the front. It makes me look as though my default 'attitude' is 'love me, love my boobies'. Which is not entirely out of kilter with the column beneath; it's as incisive a sentiment as anything I express:

At the end of the day, ladies, wouldn't it be great if we just laid eggs, like chickens? Then we'd all have just one clear-cut decision: 'I've laid an egg! Should I hatch a baby, or do I fancy an omelette?'

– Excerpt from my recent *To Breed or Not To Breed* piece.

'See how it goes, shake out your column a bit,' Miriam is telling me.

Oh. I'm offered what looks like an extra job but it's actually my existing job in a different guise. *Shake out my column* – shake off my column more like – say what you mean, Miriam.

'But I've already filed my next column,' I remind her.

'Oh yes. Sorry, tweak my memory, will you?'

'The one about the SUVs? What are they all about? You know, the anomaly of urban dwellers clogging up city roads with all these off-road four-wheel drives. What's that all about: status symbol or call of the wild? Americanisation or deeper desire to return to agrarian roots? I feign anger about it, and I'm, erm, funny. And I mention the English-as-a-Foreign-Language student I know who got knocked down by one, and also the fact that my hunky neighbour owns one; you know, the awful "he's sexy but unsound" conundrum, so it's personal.' And all the things Miriam has been nagging me to attempt since she became the editor: 'People like to read about people.' 'Make it about you.' 'Err on the side of fluff. Become the reader's ditsy friend they look forward to hearing from every week.' Every week it's the same; she feels there's something lacking in my column. Her last comment on the matter was, 'I need an Every Woman, not a left-field loon'. I think she's just priming me for the boot.

'Sounds a bit of a hackneyed topic. Don't think so. We'll run the interview in your "Attitude" slot instead, see how we get on,' she says.

Well, that puts me in my place.

'OK, will do. I wonder could you e-mail Paddy's press release and details before the interview?'

'Sure, and there should be lots of stuff on the Internet about him too.'

'Ta,' I say. Yeah, and thanks for the lead – information on the Internet? No way!

'And I need it on my desk first thing tomorrow morning,' she says.

'But tomorrow's Saturday!'

'That's the way my deadlines are for Wednesday now. Tomorrow morning, good girl.' She rings off.

'Good girl?' Apart from my mother, Miriam's the only person in the last twenty-three years who considers that an appropriate way to address me. Should I be flattered? Maybe she really thinks I'm still twelve years old? 'But Mary, you're so young-looking, so fresh, what's the secret?' I should tell her straight out: 'Miriam, you mid-thirties, me mid-thirties, enough already of the "good girls". I should have nipped the 'good girl' thing in the bud straight off, four months ago, when she took over as editor. Should have, but didn't. Maybe that's why some of my friends call me 'The Shoulda/Woulda/Coulda World Champion'. But in this case, instinctively, I've just been trying to tread lightly.

Molly Finnegan, Miriam's predecessor, was so easy to deal with. It was she who gave me my first column, 'The View from Behind', written under my pseudonym 'Tellybelly', when I was still working in RTÉ. When I lost the telly job, and 'Tellybelly' was no more, Molly kept me on and gave me 'Attitude'. But since she retired and Miriam took over, I've been on tenterhooks. I feel whatever I do it's never enough for Miriam. There's something that bugs her about me, I just don't get what it is. The dynamic between us makes me nervous. She's been steadily making changes to *Midweek* since she took over. I could be the next change in the making ...

I *can't* lose this column. It and my ten hours a week TEFL teaching constitute the bulk of my income since RTÉ gave me the boot. My other freelance writing hasn't really taken off yet, though I *nearly* got a break recently – *The Sunday Tittler* was looking for a new hackette for their 'Girl About Town' column, and I made it down to the last two.

'Girl About Town' is a 'who's who and where've they been this week' sort of thing. I'd have had to do some serious boning up on who is a *Tittler*-who. *The Tittler* is famous for its manufactured celebs, people who are famous for *The Tittler* pretending they are. Pick it up on a Sunday and you'll find yourself reading the likes of: *You'll be interested to hear that Trixie von Flynn and Trevor mac Rosencrantz-Mulhuddard jetted down to Mullingar this week to tie the knot under a dolmen, afterwards feasting on ironic bacon and cabbage. Best of luck to our favourite couple.*

Meanwhile, most of the country, like you, are thinking, 'Who the hell are these people they're on about?', but nobody seems to mind. Well-known? If they're thin and have the look of money about them, they'll do.

So, a bit of a bonkers job, really, but it would have paid better than 'Attitude' and been a lot more fun than standing in a class-room, explaining for the umpteenth time that the correct expression is eye*brow*, not eye*moustache*. Maybe the fact that I didn't get the job reflected my own doubts: is this what I *really* want to be doing? I dunno, is the answer.

Oh Lord, the twisted turn of events that have led up to me relying on something like this.

Maybe my mother is right after all: *It was your own fault you got fired from RTÉ. You shouldn't have been so cocky. Why don't you just get a proper job? Why don't you do law? You could do a conversion degree. I've sent you the prospectus. And the application form. And a cutting from the paper about Dolores Kennedy from down the road who was called to the bar there recently. She looks lovely in the wig. It's very flattering.* Yeah, well it would be, on her.

Sometimes I think I'd be happier getting away from all of this. Doing something completely different – like working with lepers. Which reminds me, I still haven't sent away for that information pack on Trócaire volunteer work. But I did buy Rory a chicken for Namibia for Christmas.

I lie on in bed, looking through a crack in the curtains at the dawning day outside. The stone cone of the spire of St Patrick's Cathedral dominates the view; its ancient beauty belittles the ugly new apartment blocks beneath. Apparently St Patrick's is built on a criss-cross of ley lines; surely those mythic energy pathways should be pumping some of the stuff right beneath where I am? Hello, Source Master of the Universe, magic oomph malfunction in Dublin 8. Please read your *Ogham* manual and rectify asap.

Streaks of yellow and pink ignite the brightening sky. It's beautiful, but I'm tired, sorry for myself, and sad that there's no big bull of a man to pull me out of this. There's supposed to be, isn't there, by this stage in the proceedings? Isn't that what men are here for, to be there? If I was firmly with a man, now is the time I'd be going, 'OK, let's do the kids thing, there's not much else on the horizon.' I could fill this emptiness with dirty nappies, the lack of sleep would put paid to any 'career worries', and my own mistakes would be completely salved by the process of producing new little people who would grow, prosper and generally do a lot better than I ever could. Reminds me of the old joke, the Mammy going 'help, help, my son *the doctor* is drowning.'

No such hilarious emergencies for me.

There is a man in my life, though: Rory. Rory loves my

uncertainties – my 'dittery culchie softness' he called it the last time we were here together. He was smacking my arse and looking for his shirt and smoking a cigarette all at the same time and who says men are no good at multi-tasking? Rory is the man I sleep with, less frequently in the last while, come to think of it. My 'shag chum' he calls me sometimes. I don't like the title. While I attempt a similar nonchalance (why?) I don't quite see it that way. The female in me wants something more; maybe it's just biology. But for whatever reasons, I've accepted 'the situation' for well over three years at this stage. We're lovers but not lovers, because the word implies 'love'. Although Rory often declares his love après climax (his, not mine most often, let's be honest) the only trouble is it's not his love for me, but for Isobel, who can't be with him openly because she's married to John, one of his best friends. He tells me all about their passionate coupling after we've 'shagged'. 'I can't bear the thought of John touching her, of them sharing the same bed. Mary, you can't imagine what I'm going through,' kind of thing. Our intimacy opens him up, about her.

It's a relief to Rory to have me as his bosom buddy: 'You've got great tits,' is the sort of intimacy he retains for me. That'll be accompanied with, for instance, him snuggling his head like a terrier between them, which is meant to be cute. And I accept it as such, in lieu of real intimacy, which if I'm honest has become an endangered experience in my life.

We have quite good sex, fairly often and we like each other. I laugh at his jokes, he thinks I'm funny, and talented, and 'come on, not fat at all' if I ask. And he believes in me: he got me into print in the first place, which, well, led to The Poison Dwarf episode, which led to me losing my budding television career, which leaves me here. Which maybe isn't a good thing overall when I think about it, but at least there's a turnover of stuff going on in my life. I'm not gathering moss.

Some might say they couldn't handle the lack of commitment, but perhaps that's exactly what attracts me. Maybe I don't want the responsibility of a man all to myself? I have all the best bits of him: the going out, the sharing a bed just for fun, keeping everything in laugh territory – the highlights of a relationship. And the only drawback is that I know he's with me like this because he loves somebody else. Or so he says. All I know for sure is that he sleeps with Isobel all over her rambling home when John's away on business and the kids are in the crèche.

'I can't tell you, Mary, you can't imagine, we just couldn't wait. In the door, straight away, we just ripped the clothes off each other. I ended up fucking her in the downstairs closet, on a bed of winter coats. I was fucking John's wife on his overcoat. What if I left a–'

Don't, please.

He turns himself on with me by recounting his adventures with her. Which is hard to take, particularly when I'm pre-menstrual and could do without the perverse undertones of our coming together. Still, he loves it when I slap his face in the throes. He thinks I'm being erotic, when mostly I'm just being good old plain pissed off. It ain't Eros, baby, it's Mars. 'That makes me soooo horny,' he'll say, the reddening shadow of my hand burning on his cheek. So horny in fact that he's taken a third lover.

He told me that recently. Don't ask me how I felt, I don't know myself. My mind just went like a television at the end of transmission: fuzzy, zinging, with the possibility that maybe it really was The End – that the confusion of inner wires had finally blown.

'I don't know how it happened. I'm so confused, what am I

doing? Thank God you're here, Mary, you're the only one I can really talk to. I couldn't tell Isobel, she'd go bananas.' That's what he said.

'What about me?' I choked.

'Oh, you're taken as given,' was how he put it, kissing my back.

Great, isn't it, I don't even have the power to make another woman jealous.

'So why are you telling *me* about your other, other woman?' I asked him.

'Just so you can never accuse me of not being upfront,' he'd said, pulling me on top of him, ending that line of enquiry. And then we made love, or whatever is the technical name for what we do together.

I haven't quite worked out yet how I feel about this new development. I'll probably see him tonight and I've been thinking vaguely of turning the whole thing on its head: asking Rory to finish with Isobel, finish with mystery third woman and ... was that what my dream was about?

Declan told me years ago that he felt women always seemed to be looking for something when they hooked up with men, always seemed to be snuffling around with a 'but will this work?' attitude, always seemed to want more than the right here and now. 'You're there thinking, *she's quite nice*, and she's already planning the carpets you'll have together,' he said.

With that gem of an insight I thought I had the inside track on men. I wasn't naturally of the *think ahead* mindset anyway, and I resolved never to be. I never saw beyond the next pint, I suppose. Was I wrong? Is it too late to start wanting more?

Oh, Rory (your very name like the sound of the sea and 'ee' of yippee rolled into one), Oh Rory, I want you, I want you – I want you to be the one I think of when I'm buying the tea (does Rory prefer Rooibos or Tesco Breakfast?) I want you to be the one I go through the torture of childbirth for (are you sure, Rory, you can handle being present? I know *I'd* rather not be, but I've no choice, ha, ha.) I want you to be the one I grow old with (I hope you don't think I'm being presumptuous, Rory, but I just went ahead and bought you a pack of incontinence pants, is that OK, dribbly?)

Now, why *him* you might well ask? I mean, how could I trust him, after Isobel and all that? Well, we've been together all this time, and naughty as he's been, he's always been scrupulously honest with me about it. Honesty is everything in my book. Trust. I do trust him. Fact is, if he asked me to marry him I would ... But why wait for him to do the asking?

There's an idea for 'Attitude' – what's with the whole Leap Year thing? Why is it only OK for women to do the asking once every four years, a one in one thousand three hundred and fifty-nine chance? Why can't we just go for it – or is that idea in the same mould as the 'DIY Sister' piece I did? Miriam, as per usual, wasn't mad about it. She berates me for being 'too earnest', for being a 'feminista' (like it's such a dirty word she can't say it in English).

'If you want to start a bra bonfire again I think you're writing in the wrong place,' she said. 'And need you be reminded that Grossard take out a regular full-page ad with us?'

CHAPTER 2

Bong, bong, bong, bong, bong, bong, bong.

The bells of St Patrick's announce the hour. I better get up. If I quickly throw on some gym gear I can make it over the road for seven fifteen spinning. Will I, won't I, will I ...

Bang, bang, bang. Next doors' bed knocks off my wall as the O'Sports have a right royal bonk, bonk, bonk to make up for the canoe tiff. Right, I'm off to the gym. Out of bed, bleary eyed, I try to source my shoes under the jumble of yesterday's clothes. I don't feel tops, probably something to do with last night's international smörgåsbord of hors d'oeuvres washed down by grape and grain.

I was at a couple of launches. I always get invited to these PR bashes, where all manner of malarkey is 'launched' into tomorrow's media (or so they hope). I suppose there's the possibility I might mention them in my column, hence the invites. But I hardly ever do and I hardly ever go, and if they read between the lines of what I actually write, I'd be the last person on anyone's 'launch' list.

Maybe I've a fanciful opinion of myself, but I can see my life taking a better path than that of a freewheeling ligger, quaffing champagne at three different events four nights a week until you get to a point where you think this is real life. Skinny PR girls making sure you're 'OK', as if you wouldn't be, what with good-looking non-nationals at every turn offering you everything from a mini sausage to caviar on a microcosm of loaf, while a posh quintet or stray harpist twiddle out classical wallpaper. Sure, each company tries to keep the whole thing 'on message' but everyone is just there for the glass and a chat. Given the name 'launch', you'd reasonably expect that the focal point should be something being projected upward – the product attached to a firework and set off to a drumroll and general applause at the very least. But no, the real surprise of a 'launch' is that the focal point of the celebration is usually a mumbling suit thanking 'the team' for working so hard on whatever it is, and everyone present for supporting same, when, let's face it, all anyone's here for is the gratis tipple and the goody bag.

Ah now, the goody bag, there's my launch yardstick: go if it looks like there'll be a good one. That's precisely why I ended up at Celtic Earth: A New Collection for The Discerning Bathroom, 6:30pm in the Merrion Hotel last night. Fancy product going free, yes please. 'Buttercup and Heather', 'Peat Smoke and Lavender', 'Dog Rose and Hay', 'Summer Hedge' – I got one of each as a soap, cologne, scrub, 'body marg' and face peel, as well as a 'Bog Water Nutritive Bath Soak'. I was happy; all I had to do was turn up, drink three Bellinis, scoff seven tiger prawns and a crab vol au vent and glance over the press release: Celtic Earth, esoteric *parfums pour la* refined nose, basically. The luxury of the Irish countryside brought to your bathroom. I grew up in the countryside and you'd be hard pushed to call anything to do with bog water or hedgerows luxury. But there you go, that's what they call spin I suppose.

I left the Celtic Earth launch before the actual launch, sneaking out with my goodies as the suit was limbering up with a few preliminary coughs into the microphone. The massive glass urns of carefully arranged whin bushes hid my escape. Ah, the whiff of the whins, I could have been out on the wild wastes of the home bog but for the fact that I was in a five-star, taupe, marble, carpet and crystal 'Ireland-is-rich-now!' hotel. I was meeting my friend Monica and had suggested Ballyhaunis Water, launching 7:30pm, The Mart Bar. No, I wasn't going there in the hope of a free litre and a half of bottled bubbling brook. I just figured there might be on-the-house beer at the bar, and that's what we fancied.

Monica was with two work colleagues; we had pints and a laugh and munched on heaps of deep fried bits with chilli dip, salmon sushi and small sausages (bit of a schizophrenic buffet, that one). We stayed on long after the suit had declared Ballyhaunis Water official: 'We're going to put the Bally up to the big boys' he proclaimed to generalised whoops from his staff. Presumably he was referring to Ballygowan; he left it to his audience to figure out the convoluted intentions of the statement.

Monica and I got quite tetchy with each other towards the end of the night; sometimes we get like that when we've had a few jars. We've never really had a straightforward 'all cards on the table' relationship. Everything's always been 'grand, grand, grand' with us, even when it hasn't been. The gentle Breege has been the neutral zone in the trio of our friendship, the butter in our pal-sandwich. Perhaps that dynamic has shifted since Breege got married, settled and pregnant and Monica and I have been cast together as the thirty-something singletons? Although I'm not *strictly speaking* 'single' in that I do have Rory. Perhaps Monica is jealous of that? Perhaps we need to talk it out? Well, we'll have the chance when we meet for dinner at Chumps this evening. Great, I hate confrontations – if that's what it's going to be.

I run across the road in my sweats, a towel tucked under my arm. It's handy that the gym is so near. It used to be a public baths; a swim 'n' scrub come-all-ye for the inner city great unwashed, by all accounts. Now you're perfectly free to enter, if you have the spondulicks, or a friend like Rory. He gave me this year's membership as a Christmas present. I wonder was he just being nice, or was he trying to tell me something?

I head downstairs to the changing rooms to dump my sweat-shirt in a locker. There's a small gang of spinning fanatics in before me, urgently pulling workout wear over sleep-heavy limbs. Suits, in shades of black to blue, and shirts in various states of white, are neatly strung on hangers in each locker. This is the zone of the go-getting woman, the one who wants the flat tum, tight buns and low resting pulse rate to help her get wherever that bit quicker. You can't help but notice that some of us look a lot tighter and fitter than others. I try not to have cardio-vascular envy, or continually compare my bod to others, but I saw a dia-gram in a magazine recently of what the perfectly formed arse should look like and I find myself automatically on the lookout for that posterior perfection since. Then the bottom I'm sizing up turns around.

'Ciara. Oh, hi,' I say.

'Hi Mary,' she smiles.

Ciara is one of the naturally fit sort, she could be living on a diet of beer and buns and still look like she'd just returned from decathlon boot-camp, yet she's in here three weekday mornings a week. (And still the curve of her bum hasn't reached that fabled arse-utopia, I was just noting.) She's an accountant.

I helped her out with a charity fun run she organised for cancer research last month – I managed to get Miriam to feature it as a 'Now' thing to do in her 'What's Then/What's Now' *Midweek* column. Apparently it tripled the number of entries. Well, you do what you can.

'You look like you need sleep more than exercise,' she tells me as we head up to the studio for the class.

'Yeah,' I agree, 'I was at a couple of press things last night, and then I went on. Ah, you know the way...'

'No, I don't,' she answers, 'I was in the office until nine last night. The only thing I was at was a profit and loss account.'

'And how was it?'

'Oh, madly exciting. I can't decide which was the best bit: the adding, the subtracting or merely the forgetting the depreciation and having to go back over the whole lot again. And yours?'

'Well, just look at this,' I tell her, posing with my bottle of 'Ballyhaunis Still'.

'I wish I had your life,' she sighs.

Yeah? You can have it, I think, but of course I don't say that.

We're in the studio. Dozza, the trainer, already has the music pumping. He's slow jogging on the spot, beside his bike, waiting for everyone to be ready.

'Come on, ladies, we haven't got all day,' he enthuses in his broad Aussie bray.

The rest of the bikes are arranged in a semi-circle around his. I chose one off to the side, out of his immediate eye-line.

'If need be, I want to die discreetly,' I explain to Ciara.

'Know the feeling,' she concurs, climbing on the bike next to mine.

'And nooaaa hiding ladies,' he adds, glancing over. You can tell by the way the tan arms are pumping in time with the music that this is going to be one of his 'no pain no gain specials'.

Dozza kicks up the music to a deafening volume and hops on his bike.

'Slow warm-up, up on those pedals, come on, ladies,' he shouts.

'R.I.P,' Ciara says.

'Amen,' is all I can manage as Dozza's 'slow warm-up' becomes a standing cycle in time with an accelerated Christina Aguilera going on about being beautiful no matter what anyone says.

'Concentrate ladies,' Dozza shouts. 'And bloke,' he adds, finally realising there's one fella in the class.

It feels virtuous to be up and out at this hour, exercising – penance for last night's million calories of alcohol and fiddly food. I feel fit, if a bit sick. A speed-beat Kylie comes on the boom box, telling us she just can't get you outta her head.

'That's exactly the way I feel about my hangover,' I puff to Ciara. But she doesn't hear me, there are more important things on her mind, like how to keep doing this and stay alive.

'Let's climb a mountain,' Dozza orders, 'take it up. Looking good, ladies. And bloke.'

Looking good? I catch a glimpse of myself in the studio mirrors: face aglow, hair a-fuzz and the shiny tight cycle trews straining with a little more than pure thigh muscle. My legs looks like two black puddings giving it welly on an exercise bike. I don't look so much fit as panicked. As if the building is on fire and I'm desperately trying to pedal my way out of here on this static bike.

I increase the resistance, and push hard into the pedals. My thighs burn, droplets of sweat drip from my forehead. I can feel my heart beat at the back of my throat. I look around. Everyone in the class is lost in their own private hell of effort.

We climb a perpetual mountain. Jennifer Lopez insists in double-time that she's just Jenny from the block, but no one could give a shite; everyone's too busy trying to stay on the right side of a coronary. Then Dozza decides we've hit the summit.

'OK, ease off, pull it back, get a drink, we're not finished yet.' Time for half a gulp of Ballyhaunis Water and we're stuck in again: a set of standing sprints, a few hillocks, a marathon, another mountain, a dash ...

'Imagine the landscape you're cycling through,' Dozza encourages. 'The trees, the paddocks. You can see the sea in the distance,' he hollers over the music. He's in Cairns in his head. I can only see rivers of molten fire and the devil poking me in the arse.

Idea for 'Attitude': Gym Obsession – Health or History? Simply an interest in the body beautiful, or bio-memory yearning to return to the physical labour of our hunter-gatherer ancestors? Americanisation or deeper desire to return to agrarian roots? Stupid idea, or incredible insight? What's the core idea there, roots or something?

'Don't fiddle with abstract ideas in your column, Mary, please,' Miriam has said to me in the past, 'you only sound pseudo. Bed what you're saying in real, tangible things – like moisturiser.'

She'd rather something like a thousand words on Celtic Earth Burdock Body Scrub for next week: *Make your bum beautiful with a butt ugly plant*. You need a degree in being An Ageing Male Spouter to get to posit anything approaching A Big Idea in *The Irelander*.

'Ripper work, ladies. And bloke,' Dozza exalts us at the end of the class.

'Good start to the day. I'm completely exhausted after that,' I tell Ciara.

'Me too,' she agrees, although she doesn't look it.

As I leave her to shower and change in the gym, I ask her what she has planned for the weekend. She tells me 'work'.

'All work and no play Ciara ... ' I remind her.

'All mortgage and no money,' she laughs in reply.

'Enjoy,' I say as I wave goodbye. Well, if you will insist on the extravagance of living in an actual house, what do you expect? I, on the other hand, live simply, in a box. A box subsidised by my brother. But not everyone is as lucky as me.

I leave the gym at a sluggish jog, dodging the manic morning traffic as I cross the street. I nearly floor an elderly gent returning from Londis on Patrick Street with *The Irelander* and a packet of Woodbines.

'Sorry, sorry,' I puff. *The more haste, the less speed*, my father's voice comes to mind. 'The more speed the less haste,' elderly gent says. I've seen him before; he's one of the residents of the men's hostel opposite the gym. He shuffles off in his slippers and his holey jumper.

The phone's ringing as I come back into the apartment. I don't answer. Mammy is the only one who phones me on the landline. The last thing I need now is an interminable 'You know what I was thinking you could do' conversation: half an hour or more of me convincing Mammy that everything couldn't be better with me, and no, don't worry, I don't regret that the Four Courts isn't more central to my existence. I let the phone ring out, and it rings again when I'm in the shower.

'I don't hear you,' I say out loud, pumping Frizz-Ease into my hair, trying to tame my Celtfro. 'Head 'o' pubes' Rory calls me.

Out of the shower, I make a pot of coffee and turn on my computer to check e-mails, *google* Paddy Finn, and make some notes for that interview. As I wait for it to boot up I jot down a To Do list. I read an interview with Catherine Zeta Jones in which she said that's what Michael does every morning. A list. And that why he's A-List. That's the secret of his success. He is the man with everything: fame, fortune, success, the beautiful wife and a house in Pontypridd or wherever. So all hail The Daily List. If a list means I've clean knickers the next morning then it's worth it. Do laundry. And then you do. That feels like success. Maybe I'm ambition deficient, but there were ample clean knickers in the drawer this morning, and that's good enough for me. More or less.

Actually, my list for today makes me sound quite interesting – a leg wax followed by TV appearance on 'Afternoon Stew'; Paddy Finn interview, The Westbury, then dinner at Chumps and Babette Manion's opening at The Project. Not bad, Mary.

I check my in-box. Miriam hasn't forwarded that press release. There are two new messages, one my daily astrology forecast. It's American and I love it; even when things are bad they're good – the planets must come up differently when charted from the States. Today I need love, but I should wait until tomorrow, I shouldn't buy anything electrical, or sign a contract, but I should remember it's the first day of the rest of my life and I am a warm, viable human being. All right!

There's also a mail alerting me to new 'winks' from the dating website I joined late one night recently. Curious, I click onto www.eire-pairing.ie and enter my password. Two guys find me 'interesting' according to the generic message: *Loverman* is 'looking for someone who wants to be loved like a woman, respected like a lady and treated like a queen.' I'd suggest Freddie Mercury, if he was still around.

Next there's *Dubulike*: he considers himself 'above average attractive'. His photo shows a receding hairline, moustache and Horslips t-shirt. He's divorced, has two children 'not living with me', and 'enjoys a gargle' and 'a singsong'. Imagine, me, stepmom to Dubulike's sprogs, the terraced life, the ballad sessions of a Sunday night and the battered sausage on the way home. Oh God, the great grey mudflats of most men.

I always thought I'd end up with someone like Sebastian. He was the first man I ever loved. I was ten and he was the homosexual with the teddy in 'Brideshead Revisited'. I had no problem with Sebastian's predilection for cuddly toys and men. The former seemed normal and the latter didn't matter because what did I know? I just plastered his newsprint picture all over my bedroom wall and said goodnight to him every night and hello to him every morning until he became fixed as my ideal, my angel. He was magically beautiful, and I knew that was the kind of man I wanted when I grew up and I knew I was right because my brother Cormac was totally in love with him too.

Rory is the spit of Sebastian.

I've just brought up the google page for my research when the phone rings. It's Monica. Oh no, exposition time? I'm not in the mood, it's too early, and who's going to say 'sorry for being cranky last night' first. Not me ...

'Hi?' I answer, with a 'who is it?' inflection, pretending I don't know it's her.

'Hi, Mary, it's me. Listen, I have to be brief because I'm in a hurry, but Breege had her baby late last night, boy, seven pounds. Sean can't make it in this morning and I'm up to my tonsils; I wonder would you be free? Say you're family and you can get in; she's a bit teary.'

'Breege had her baby! That's amazing. I thought it wasn't due for another couple of weeks?'

'I know, it's brilliant, isn't it? Sudden, premature, but everything fine. Can you go?'

'When did you find out?' I ask, deliberately ignoring her no-emotion, busy-busy-business-tone. She has this habit of phoning up with the cold tone when she's in work-mode and wants every-thing to be snippy snappy. I seem to oscillate between being 'friend' and 'item on the agenda'. Breege, Monica and I have been friends since college. One of us has had a baby! Shouldn't we be weeping tears of womanly indulgence across the phone at each other?

'7, 7:30 this morning. Sean texted me. I called Breege straight away, just spoke with her now. I know she'd like some company.'

Do you now? Seeing as half the time you seem to respond to the world as if you were a machine, how do you know? Maybe Breege is bonding with her baby, sitting there sore-bummed but happy, thinking, wow, look at the little mini-me. That's what I'd imagine having a child is like anyway.

I glance at my mobile. There's the message, sent to me too –

It's a boy! 7lbs! Born midnight. Luv S & B X

And of course I'm dying to see Breege and little whatever-he's-called, but now it's like Monica is organising me – yet again.

Feck it, I just say yes.

Yes, Monica, we both know that your schedule is more inflexible than mine; that'll be the proper job. Yes, of course I'm free. I'm freelance. It's in the title. Now I'll have to stop off in Grafton Street to buy a present as well, but hey, what's life about, if not life?

'Good,' Monica says, 'I've got to dash, see you in Chumps later.'

'Yeah, 6:20, see you then.'

'6:35 I think we said?'

'6:20.'

'6:35. Look, I have to go. See you then. Ciao.'

She's gone.

We *had* said 6:20, I wrote it down. It's there in my diary. I was right.

I call Breege to congratulate her. It's strange that Monica got there first, generally I would say that I'm closer to Breege than Monica. I feel like my 'first girlfriend to say hurray for the baby' rights have been violated! What am I like? In any case I get her message minder, and leave a voice mail telling her I'll be there shortly and I'm over the moon, of course.

I close down the computer, grab the ironing board from the hot press, set it up in my lounge-cum-dining-cum-utility-cum-only decent bit of space in the flat and set to the hated chore. I can't look creased on telly this afternoon, particularly since it's my first time out there since the 'Poison Dwarf' episode. I flick on the radio.

'Well, Bryan, when I lost the leg I had to accept the hurdling days were over, so I just went looking for another challenge ...' someone is saying. 'But what a challenge you chose ...' goads Byran Pratt, radio host and rising television star, spurring the interview along. He's talking to a one-legged woman who rode a llama up the length of Peru. It's one of those heart-warming tales that's meant to encourage you with the strength of the human spirit, but ends up making you feel inadequate. Strength of the human spirit? A woman with a mere single leg learns to ride an obscure herbivore against all the odds and I can't even be arsed pressing this shirt properly. She hopped up Machu Picchu while I limit myself to front, collar and cuffs?

Dressed, I down two mugs of coffee and scoff an old fig roll and half a tub of yoghurt. I've been meaning to do a proper shop for, ohh, months at this stage. I did the questionnaire in 'You are what you eat' and according to the author I should be dead.

I exit the apartment, hair a damp fuzz, pants in need of an iron, make-up simple, a smear of gloss on the lips, a touch of definition on the eyebrow. Hell, the dishevelled look is in at the moment, I just did a piece about that for the 'Chic Sister' column of *Irish Nurse*: 'Why Creases will be Hot this Summer.'

The editor loved it. Well, good news for the average underpaid, overworked nurse propping up the shambles of our health service: take some pressure off, chuck away the ironing board. I wish everybody were crumpled, always, all the time. Then I'd fit in.

Are YOU bikini fit? a window display asks me as soon as I get into Grafton Street.

None of your business.

Baby gift being top of the agenda, I find myself entering the gilded portals of Brown Thomas. People are always saying that Penneys have a great selection of cheap baby whatnots, but if it's a present you're looking for, a stripy BT's bag with in-built black ribbon and an acre of tissue paper shows you care. Not that Breege thinks that way herself, she's from Sligo.

Straight in the door and I'm lost in a half-acre of handbag. Is there some handbag voodoo I'm missing, some bag language I'm not privy to? I find myself wondering, as I get momentarily way-laid by the display of mad leather. Maybe there's an 'Attitude' in this?

–Bag Ladies –

If the choice, 'quality' and expense of handbag available on your doorstep is a measure of SUCCESS! then it's definite: Ireland is truly well clear of the 800-year doldrums. But look at these things! What do these saddle-shaped yokes covered in rhinestone and feathers say? 'Hey gringo, I'm a cow-girl kinda gal. I'm yee-haw mighty good craic but I sure is into my bling. And if you, Mr Mighty Fine Sir, have the kind of silly loola this thing costs, well buckaroo off and hog-tie me the matching four figure looks-like-a-pony vanity case, and the limited-edition weekender with real stallion-hoof handle, complimentary tomahawk, and in-built whinnying alarm, and you can ride me away into the sunset, and that is an offer.

Should I run that past Miriam? Don't think so.

I make for the escalator and am distracted by the offer of a smelly squirt: Eau de Barbotte, the new scent from Brigitte Bar-botte. The perfume girl gives me a spray and the lowdown on the aroma components. 'L'essence de Brigitte Barbotte?' I think, while she's spieling away. Surely that should be base of cats' pee and dog pooh with notes of donkey dandruff? But, hey, she's only doing her job. So, 'Thanks anyway,' I say. She nods, already on the lookout for another lady to spray, a tomcat claiming territory. Brigitte would be proud.

Upstairs, I find myself scooting around designer wonderland. Yes, I know that the newborn malarkey is probably not hidden under the Dolce e Gabbana, but who could pass and not glance at that glittery dress, stop to feel the silky texture, to rub the nubbly diamonds on the buttocks, to be awed that one human being would design that for another, and that they'd both take each other seriously enough for hard cash to be involved? €1189 for instance. Who indeed could call themselves a woman and not be drawn to the tasselled, studded Versace ensemble, noting how one instantly feels less than the wearer, even if it's only a mannequin. Marni, Armani, Missoni, Ungaro, they all sound like sauce, and how apt, they're all designed for linguini-thin women, women who wouldn't touch pasta in a fit. Oh the rich-but-starving irony.

This is another world. A lovely, hushed, carpeted perfumed world, fashion-silly, fake and forbidden for me who feels rich when I'm only, say, two, three hundred in the red. And yet I'm totally at home: hello Lainey, hello Stella, hello Issey, hello Max. What am I doing? I had one goal in here: baby present. Please pursue.

Then, like dirt to a Dyson, I'm sucked across the carpet. Red letters pulse before me, independent will atomises: SALE. There's a lingerie sale, I have to, I cannot pass. This is my version of freelance: that at 9:45am on a wet Friday morning my scheduled research session, rescheduled at the last minute to a hospital visit, rerouted through a consumer thicket, has become me topless in a BT's dressing room, lacing some sort of basque yoke onto my torso. The laces take twenty minutes to adjust over excess belly, the basque buckles out all over the place as if it's repulsed by the thought of being mine, but at a major squeeze it looks fantastic because it has to; it's reduced from €145 to €35.

10:09, delighted, I watch as Eileen (according to her name tag) reverentially wraps the folded basque in crisp thick tissue paper, sealing it with an oblong sticker of the Brown Thomas insignia. This is not mere undies at a knockdown, this is a veritable gift to your higher self. Thanks, Mary. You're welcome, Mary. Eileen delicately ties the ribbons on my carrier bag and hands it to me.

'Enjoy your underwear,' she says. What does she think I am going to do with it, eat it?

'Thanks,' I say, 'I will.'

Who's it for anyway, Rory, or Mr Someday He'll Come Along? Feck it, why does it need justifying, won't it look perfect under that black shirt I got for a fiver in Dunnes? Now, where's the baby stuff?

'Have you any suggestions for what I might buy a newborn? Something special,' I turn back and ask Eileen. She looks like a woman who would knows these things.

'Newborn, is it? You know, I always think it's lovely to actually buy a present for the mother; everyone will be getting stuff for the baby. Spoil the mother with something instead, after what she's just been through.' Hurry or no hurry, she's conspiratorially sharing her lady wisdom with me, here in her harem of knickers. And a brilliant idea it is too. What was I expecting to get for a newborn in BTs anyway, diamante nappies?

'I didn't think of that. Excellent. Thanks,' I say, automatically scanning a row of g-strings next to me. I don't think so. It doesn't take much imagination to conclude that an after-birth mum won't be pulling on a lacy string.

As if she can see what I'm thinking, Eileen suggests something cosmetic.

'A luxurious cream. John Joe McLeod Jojoba, that would be a gorgeous gift, bottom of the escalator, on the left.'

I arrive at the John Joe McLeod counter and leave in the same second. A small J.J. Jojoba costs the price of my weekly shop. Enough already, John Joe, Manhattan's gone to your head. Apparently he's some effeminate lad from Tullamore who never fitted in, but found himself when he went to America and ended up rubbing moisturiser of his own making on some superstar's chapped chin. She was so delighted with his smoothing lubricants that they're now index-linked to platinum.

Cosmétique Monique Monique? She looks marginally cheaper. Monique2 is a woman from Paris who believes real beauty comes from inside, and from secret ingredients distilled only in Laboratoire Monique Paris * New * York * Rome * Moscow * Manchester. Her products are covered in French, the lingua franca of pampered skin, so they must be good. For instance, there's *Essence Fermeté Pour Les Seins* and *Fluide Défatigent Revitalisant*, basically saggy boob essence and fluid for the haggard. I've wasted precious minutes ploughing through these unctions when it suddenly hits me: I've got a whole heap of token toiletries at home, from last night and other cosmetic launches. Why didn't I just bring some of that for Breege? Feck it, too late now. I run across the street to M&S and buy her a melon, a bunch of grapes, and a bottle of sparkling boysenberry juice, whatever that is. It's the thought that counts.

On the way out – shame, I'm a wastrel – a fake sparkler catches my eye. I'm not one for rings, I find them irritating, but I have to have it. If it was the real McCoy it would be coming under the hammer at say, oh, five grand at least, so it's a snip, on sale, €3. I put it in my pocket for tonight. Maybe me wearing it will give Rory ideas?

CHAPTER 3

'Holles Street, please,' I ask as I scrunch into a cab at the top of Grafton Street.

We creep off into the mid-morning traffic.

'The Jerry Lee doesn't seem to have done much for the congestion, what?' the taxi driver comments in a conversational shout.

'I'm sorry?' I say.

'The ould Daniel Day, supposed to bring less cars into the city centre. Me hole, what?'

Daniel Day? Daniel Day Lewis? He wasn't supposed to bring his car into the city? I'm not following him. Then I get it, he's referring to The Luas, the light railway. I thought that was old news by now. Obviously not to Grumps behind the wheel.

'Oh, the Luas, the Jerry Lee, Daniel Day, oh, I see, very funny, yes. No, no it doesn't seem to have lessened city centre traffic at all. It must drive you nuts.'

I figure if I get him into a monologue on his feelings about traffic in general I won't have to say another word until we get to Holles Street. It's only down Dawson Street, and right along Nassau, straight through to Merrion Square. Five minutes, not factoring the aforementioned traffic, of course.

'Oh, Jaysus, ya can't imagine, sometimes I feel like just smashing me head through the windscreen, sometimes I think to meself if only I had a Kalashnikov I'd ...' and he's off. I tune out.

I'm looking at my stuff. I can't just give Breege an M&S plastic bag of fruit, can I? Quick switch, lingerie goes in plastic shopper, goes into vast handbag. Fruit and fizzy drink get the tissue paper and BT's bag treatment. There, not quite the fancy gift I had envisaged, but it's the thought ...

'... you know, like a tank, just smashing and crushing all the cars out of the way, people inside, the lot, especially the culchies. Sorry, missus, you're not a culchie yourself, are you?'

'Yes,' I answer what I take is the end of the taxi driver's rant, 'I am indeed what you might call a culchie.'

Just to get him away from the violence and the stereotyping of his fellow countrymen, I ask him has he ever heard of Paddy Finn. Vox of the populus. Surprise, surprise, he has big fat opinions about Paddy, too.

'The comic? Wouldn't be my cup of tea. Saw him on 'The Late Late Show'. Giving out about the church. Shure that's not comedy, it's too easy. Nah, gimme the likes of Bob Fatty Blue any day, or Bazz Canning, have you seen him? €5:40 please, now he's good.'

We've arrived at the hospital. He prattles on as I pay.

'What was this his show was again? *How's The Big Bazoomas, Bridie?* Ah, now that was class. We were in the front row and he called my wife a right manky slapper. I swear to God she wet herself.'

Well, on that note of your wife's incontinence I take my leave of you, kind sir I should say.

'And have you seen his last video, *How's The Big Bubbly Bouncy Balls, Ya Bollix?*

'No. Must look out for that, it sounds lovely. Bye now, mind you don't run down any culchies,' I tell him, as I bang the door shut.

While I'm standing at the hospital reception, an overripe mother-to-be shuffles in, urgent but slow, heavy-bellied, heavy breathing, supported on either side by anxious relatives. I move aside to allow her to the desk before me. It's all in a day's work for the guys behind the desk; without the blink of an eye a wheelchair is called for and she is calmly reassured. Meanwhile, she leans on the desk, eyes tightly shut, panting in agony. Within two minutes she's been whisked off to the labour room, the anxious father in her wake. The other relation is left stranded alone in the foyer for the tense wait. She's an older woman, the mother of one of the parents-to-be, no doubt.

'Best of luck,' I say to her, the spontaneous words reaching out like the touch of a hand to her arm. *Best of luck* is not the most appropriate sentiment perhaps, but she nods and half-smiles, thankful, I think, for the shared acknowledgement of the intensity of the whole thing. Women give birth every minute of every hour of every day all over the world; it's as average as rainfall, but that doesn't detract from the fear and anticipation that surrounds each and every one of these many miracles. It literally is life and/or death. This place makes me uneasy.

It's my turn at the desk.

'Hi, I'm here to see Breege Madigan. She had a little boy last night?' I address the receptionist.

Ahh, Breege Madigan who had the little boy last night, as opposed to the Breege Madigan who pushed a bloody six-foot rugby player out between her legs. My God, that was a difficult birth. He's now stretched across twelve cots in intensive care. All this fear and anticipation is making me giddy.

'It's outside visiting hours,' the security/receptionist answers.

'Sorry, I'm family. I'm her sister,' I say. 'It's her first child. She's alone. She'd like someone with her at this time.'

I add on incremental statements until he cuts across me with an 'OK'. They're strict here, I suppose you have to be, it's a busy public hospital. I'm directed to the postnatal ward. I do the two flights of stairs two steps at a time and I'm there, panting through the glass of the locked ward door with big hello-let-me-in eyes.

'Breege Madigan? I'm her sister, sister,' I say to the ward sister when she opens it. After another 'it's outside visiting hours' negotiation, I get through. The spiel this time is that I've travelled a long way, Breege is about to get out and I'm here to help her pack, and she's quite emotional remembering the seven miscarriages on the path to this successful baby ...

'Fifth door down on the right,' I'm informed before my list of made-up excuses gets any more complicated.

I'm reminded of convent school: the smudge-coloured linoleum, the stain-coloured walls, the bleached grubbiness, the Victorian austerity. I poke my head around the door. Breege is the only patient in the two-bed room, alone with her baby. She's sitting up in bed, her thick short hair a matted bonnet about her flushed and tired face. She holds the sleeping child in her arms, staring at him with a concentrated expression I cannot name. It's new. Different. It's all different now.

'Hi, Breege,' I half whisper.

'Mary, Mary you're so good to come. Monica said you couldn't wait. Come in, come in.'

'Ahh,' I say. 'He's gorgeous,' before I've even seen him. That's what you're supposed to say, isn't it? All I've seen is hospital blanket, it's white, machine-knitted, no doubt, but looks hand-knit, it looks soft and kindergarteny. Ahhh.

I move to hug Breege, and turn to take in the little fella. Eyes jammed shut, little nose a squashed button, a perfect tiny puckered mouth. His diminutive fingers play air piano. I know the world is full of them, but he's miraculous. This is Breege's baby, I can't believe it. I've known her nearly half my life, and ...

'Oh, Breege,' is all I can say.

We sit in silence for a while.

The other day, sorting through some old photographs, I came across a pack from the Greek island-hopping holiday we took together at the end of the summer of our final exams. I'm reminded of them again now. There we three were, as free as a breeze: Monica, Breege and I on our mopeds in Paros, the strong tanned sticks of our legs like something from a catalogue. Breege and I laughing into the camera, foregrounded by massive umbrellaed cocktails – that was Mykonos. There was me with some foreign-looking fella, his arm around me, his eyes down my shirt, while Monica looks on with an expression of bafflement and vague disgust. That was Amorgos, I seem to recall. 'Stop grinning at every Greek geek we pass. They take it as a come-on', I remember Monica saying to me, while Breege laughed and said 'so what' – her default comment on everything. So what indeed, I had the time of my life that summer. The youth of us – we looked as if we knew everything – and if there *was* something else, when we found out it'd be no bother to us. If only we'd known. It was all there to see in the snaps: the comparison between then and now. I felt melancholy looking at them. All I needed was the mammy from the tea ad to walk in and go 'ah, here, have a cup of Barrys'.

It's on the tip of my tongue to mention some of this to Breege, to share the reminiscence of the Greek sojourn before we dove into adult selves. But I don't, of course. Here she is with her new-born, her first born. She wouldn't get sentimental over a few twelve-year-old photographs, not now. She's not looking back. She's onto the next natural thing. Fleetingly, I have the strange feeling of having been left behind in a photograph.

What do I say? Breege looks up from the mesmerising face of her baby and sees the faraway look in my eyes.

'Ah,' she says, delighted at the emotion her motherhood has brought up in me. She rubs my arm, Mammy of the world now.

'I'm so happy for you,' I say.

'I know,' she whispers.

'Have you decided on a name?' I ask quietly.

'Malachy.'

Malachy is not the kind of name that works well in a whisper. Malachy is more the kind of name you hear in a shout, the shout of a hurling coach from the sideline, say, as in:

'Malachy, ya big fucker, will you feckin' mark the man, mark him, with your stick, ya dumb ox. Maaalaccchy!'

'Malachy,' I whisper back. 'That's a lovely name. Lovely. How did you chose that?'

'Pat's maternal grandfather was a Malachy. They were very close. He gave him his first hurley.'

'Ahhh,' I say.

'Would you like to hold him?' she whispers.

No, not really. I'm nervous of tiny babies – what if I drop him? What if he spontaneously combusts in my arms?

'Great, can I?' I say. She gently passes him over. I take him in my arms. The bulk of him is blanket, he's impossibly small, a scrap of a thing. He breathes in fierce tiny breaths, life determined to have its way with him. I silently wish him a long and happy one. You can't help but think about the way the world will batter the innocence out of him. He's so vulnerable right now.

If he were mine I'd want to dress him in an anti-gravitational armoured bubble suit until he'd reached the stage where he's fast enough to run away, or stand up for himself. By which time I'd have had him trained in the ancient Eastern martial arts of control, discipline, inner-self and being able to beat the crap out of anyone who crosses you. Either that or I'd just do it for him myself. That's what I'd be like if I had one of these: 'Anyone messes with this baby here, EVER, he messes with me.'

I catch Breege looking at me. It's that look, isn't it, I think to myself. The look of the married thirty-something mother, regarding her unmarried and childless friend holding the newborn; the look of pity; the look of 'maybe someday you can have this too'; the look of, let's face it, an inverted, 'lucky me!'

Come on, Breege, you know me. Why will no one believe me when I say I don't want to have children? Apart from the bloody pain of it, look at us: the world is heaving with us, we're pushing nearly every other living thing off the planet, and still people look at you like you are a freak if you say you have no desire to add to the glut.

If you don't want kids it's either men sniff you're weird and won't go near you with their fizzing sacs, or you're a wanton bachelorette too sybaritic to get stuck into steaming-nappyland.

And either way you're going to end up mad, because you had no one to talk to in your latter years, and die alone because you tripped on your Zimmer frame and couldn't reach the phone. I don't want to make people just so I'm not alone when I'm old.

Still, I wonder, should I be feeling some *innate* mammal-envy here? I don't. But it throws up a million other questions. Like, am I normal?

'How was the birth?' I ask her.

'You don't want to know,' she says.

'OK,' I say, thinking she doesn't want to talk about it. But no, it's not that.

'Really, Mary, I mean it. You don't ever, ever want to know about this, unless you have to go through it yourself.'

'No, I do. Tell me,' I ask.

'I can't. It was pain beyond pain, on a scale of one to ten, I'd give it a fifty. And then it got worse, just before the end. I wouldn't be surprised if Sean finds he has a burst eardrum from my screams.'

'How many hours of that?'

'Five at least.'

'And no epidural?'

'No.'

'Well, you must be proud of that.'

'I can't answer that question right now,' she says.

'But you're glad you had it in hospital, I hope?' I continue.

Breege had wanted to do it in the house, in a birthing pool. But Sean was afraid of the mess; he's just put in new maple floors. And then the hospital said because it was her first and she was in her thirties she'd have to come in. She was still determined to have as little medical intervention as possible.

Monica thought she was mad. 'Breege can be such a hippy sometimes,' she said to me. 'Personally I don't get it – why not be knocked out if need be, that's what I'd want, anyway. Knock me out for the whole nine months! No, leave me in a coma 'til it's toilet trained! Not that I'll ever be in the situation. No fruit of my womb, for sure.'

'Yes, in the end I was', Breege admits. 'To be honest, Mary, at one stage I thought I was literally going to *die*. I'm serious. I felt like I couldn't breath through another contraction. I was saying to the midwife after, is this normal, is this what it's like for everyone?'

'And she said?'

'Yes. Of course. This is the deal. What I want to know is, why didn't our mothers tell us? They never really told us anything, did they?'

'Mmm, I suppose it was the done thing to just bite your tongue off and keep schtum,' I laugh, feeling a sudden pang of guilt about my mother. Who was it said, 'when you have children, you instantly forgive your parents everything'?

'I think it'll be epidurals all round when I go again, Mary.'

'You're going to go again? Already on the cards?' I love the way Irish mothers refer to having another one as 'going again', as if it's a fabulous holiday destination they've discovered.

'Oh yes,' she says, stroking Malachy's tiny head. It's smaller than her hand. 'I can't deprive him of his little brother or sister, his gang.'

I have an image of Breege with her teenage children, me jetting into the room from whatever exotic location my single self-concern has taken me, she saying, 'oh, look, my lovelies, it's Aunty Mary'. Is that who I'm setting myself up to be? Is it a choice, or something else?

'Oh, I almost forgot. I got you a little something.' Balancing

Malachy carefully in the crook of my arm, I reach down and hand her the BT's bag of fruit.

She unwraps the folds of black tissue paper. 'Trust you to be different, Mary. What is this now, designer fruit?' she says, smiling at my offering.

'Yeah, it's the new Dolce e Gabbana *essentials* line,' I laugh. 'Only the best for you, Breege. To be honest, I couldn't think of anything better in a hurry ...'

'Oh, for God's sake, don't worry. You were more than gener-ous when I had my shower. Anyway, it's your being here that matters.'

Malachy begins to cry, in shrill little gulping yelps.

'Besides, he's the best gift anyone ever got. Come here, my little man,' she says, delicately taking him from me.

She produces a boob.

'Breast-feeding?' I ask.

'Trying,' she answers, as, breasts akimbo, she manoeuvres a nipple into the new mouth. Little Malachy slobbers blindly as he attempts to latch on. I'm reminded of Rory.

'I should go,' I say, 'I'm on 'Afternoon Stew' this afternoon, around quarter to three, if you're near a television.'

'Don't know, I'll try. I might be getting out this afternoon. They still haven't decided, what with Malachy making an early entrance and my tear and stitches. I've a third degree in my you-don't-want-to-know-where. And thanks for coming in at such short notice, Mary; it sounds like you have a lot on. Sean was going to pop in, but he had to meet a client. Monica said she'd be along, then at the last minute she had to go to the studio. To be honest, I'm glad it was you that could come, Mary, and not Monica. Some-times she can be so ... you know.'

'I know.'

We pause to allow what we haven't said settle.

'You didn't have to, you know. Monica being over-conscientious again, as usual,' Breege continues.

'Yeah,' I say, 'no bother. Monica or no Monica, I would have been here.' And it was true; it was just the way that Monica imposed it on me like a duty that I resented.

Breege is still force-feeding nipple to her baby when there's a knock on the door.

'Hello, hello, Breege. Breege, are you in there?' a voice calls out.

Breege covers her feeding cleavage as best she can.

'Come in,' she calls.

Two smart oldies enter.

'Dorothy! Pat! You shouldn't have come all the way in. Now, I told you not to, you're very bold!' Breege exclaims.

It's Sean's parents. I met them at Breege and Sean's wedding three and a half years ago. It was the summer I'd met Rory, he came along as my 'guest'. It was in a castle down the country and we all stayed over. Pat, tipsy at the end of the night, took me aside to tell me Rory was a grand fella, and he hoped I'd be the next up the aisle. 'Ah now, Pat,' I recall saying to him, 'I don't know if I'm the tie-the-knot type. The future's too big a place to settle on one patch.' I was tipsy too, but not so tipsy that I didn't notice he was taken aback at my remark.

'Oh, shure it takes all sorts I suppose,' he half-laughed, before sidling away.

My remark had surprised myself – is that what I really thought?

'*In vino veritas*,' I commented to the suit of armour standing next to me. Was it just the drink, or did the visored head really nod back in agreement?

'Shure wild horses wouldn't have kept us from coming to meet the first grandfella. But we nearly didn't manage to get past the Gestapo at the door; they've only given us a minute, so let's be having him,' Pat tells Breege. He averts his eyes as she tries to discreetly remove Malachy from her breast. Even though he's a farming man himself, no one likes to think of their in-law as a heifer, do they? I help his distraction with a quick hello, and wave a quiet goodbye to Breege.

'Arra musha, look at the little fella,' Pat is saying as I exit. '*Dia dhuit*, Malachy Madigan, you'll carry the name. Good man, fair play to you.'

'He's carrying both sides in his name now ... ' their voices follow me down the hall.

I walk slowly, stopping to search for a tissue. There's a string of scraggly toilet roll in my jacket pocket. I have a good blow. Head together, feeling better, a nurse comes along.

'Ahh, you'll be all right,' she says, 'newborns have that effect on women. Sometimes.'

'Hay fever, actually,' I answer, 'always bad this time of year, err, April.'

She looks at me like she knows something I don't, and walks off.

I snuffle-up, gather my bags and head on.

CHAPTER 4

It's 11:25, I've twenty minutes to get to J'♥ Moi, so I'll walk. The
drizzle has given way to a moist greyness. You can catch a note of
spring in the air. Trees are budding in Merrion Square park,
there's a randy edge to the birds pastorale; you just can intuit the
increase in residential property prices. I walk along the railings,
heading up toward Baggot Street. This is a lovely part of Dublin. I
could contextualise it for you historically now, or from a literary
point of view if you were a visitor with a head for that kind of
stuff: that's where Michael Collins got on his bike, that's where
Joyce muddied his spats, that's where Oscar Wilde had a witti-
cism. But I wouldn't be one for cycling around dressed as a turn-
of-the-last-century butcher boy, having kidneys for breakfast and
impenetrable prose for tea. What I always recall when I'm walking in this area is an argument I had with some eejit I was seeing
one time. He stormed off, I was dying for a pee, it was late and
there was no one around, so I went in between two cars parked
just there, pulled my knickers down and was in full desperate
flow when he came back. Oh God, when I think about it! I heard
his footsteps come towards me and then retreat. Somehow we
just never called each other again. I see him around all the time,

we say 'hi'. I'm sure when he looks at me he just sees a big bottom mouthing hello at him. Dublin's like that. It's your own personal history, not the hypothetical Dedalus-diddly-do-da one, that's always in your face.

Beep beep. A car salutes me. Some guy I know waving behind the wheel. I wave back. Can't remember his name, but I think I snogged him once. See what I mean – Dublin can be awfully friendly.

My phone rings.

'HI,' booms a voice.

'Hiya Declan.'

'Can you do an E&Q L?'

'An E&Q L?

'Early and quick lunch.'

'Erm, yeah, sure.'

'Say an hour and ten starting from NOW.

'Sure.'

'BAGELUSCIOUS?'

'Sure.'

'Are you SURE?'

'Sure.' I'd rather lunch alone and go over my notes from *Trash the Pants,* the book I'm reviewing later on 'Afternoon Stew', but I'm hearing what he's not saying.

'Sure I'm sure,' I reiterate. 'Hey, you've got a pitch today. Are you sure you have the time?'

'NO! So I'll see you there at what, 12:50? OK for you?'

'12:50.'

'I am ETERNALLY INDEBTED to toi.'

'I know.'

Then he's gone. That's Declan. He's a writer, sorry, copywriter:

different universe. Declan is sensitive, highly strung, poetic, creative – all the things that make him very good and very bad for the job. Success and panic attacks in equal measure.

'I'm just too creative to be a creative,' he's been saying of himself recently. Declan would love to get out of advertising. Declan would hate to lose his job. He's an intelligent, pragmatic man. Those two desires can co-exist quite unhappily in his head. He's not just passionate about words, he's passionate about nice restaurants. And wine. And stuff. Stuff costs. He knows that. He's got it all worked out, except he hasn't.

I met Declan on a creative writing workshop in Monaghan, when I'd just moved back from England. He said he was 'working on some poems'. That used to be his thing: The Poetry. It being hardly a career move, he segued into The Copywriting, thinking that both skills would blend. Anyway, the upshot is he hasn't really written a verse in years, but he has produced award winning campaigns. He used to enjoy it, but recently he's been going on bitterly about how it's all changed: 'It's not the being creative, it's the being on time that matters now.'

Perhaps his disatisfaction has more to do with the fact that he split up with his long-term, Maureen, four years ago. She was a nurse, not a woman of the quill. That was what Declan liked about her at first, he told me, her down to earth difference from him and his writerly worries. It was also what began to niggle him. For example, the time he suggested they attend a literary festival one long weekend, and her immediate response was, 'For God's sake, I've been up to my armpits in bed pans for the last yonks, I'm not in the mood for any more shite'.

Anyway, no worries, Declan. She met and fell in love with a thatcher while on a walking weekend in the Burren. Within a year she'd moved down to Clare and married him. Hurtful, when you factor in that Declan thought they'd only been having a 'trial' separation at the time, and he'd used the separation to work out that actually he was ready to marry her.

He'd even got her name tatooed on his belly, in Laos, where he went on his own for a fortnight to 'find himself'. All he found out was that he didn't like travelling solo, and he was allergic to tattoo ink. He came back with a belly button like a flourescent buoy. Meanwhile, Turlough was weaving the roof he and Maureen would live under. Declan didn't really cop on to it until he received the 'Maureen and Turlough cordially invite you to' notice. 'He's even a wizz on the accordian,' he discovered to his disgust at the trad reception. Personally I didn't get the jealously there, but the jilted mind works in mysterious ways. 'Take up the squeeze box yourself if you're so upset' I said to him, which made him laugh. I don't know what he was thinking: maybe if I master a few speedy jigs she'll have me back?

To add injury to insult, he couldn't risk getting the sensitive tattoo fully removed, so he just had to get it painfully re-made into something else. Now Maureen is pregnant with her second child and she's working on a novel about a nurse who meets a cabinet maker while climbing The Reek, and she ends up moving down to Mayo and marrying him. He builds her the drawers to put her knickers in.

Perhaps that's the key to Declan's now constant moan about 'getting out' and 'moving on'. He feels he's been left behind. And betrayed, because the novel is also about the technical writer she abandoned in Dublin. *Finding Real Life* it's called, due out in autumn. You can just imagine the sort of thing:

Claire's boot became stuck in the rocks. She felt her ankle

twinge. Instinctively she knew her left anterior talofibular liga-
ment was torn. Flip! It seemed senseless to call out, there was no
one else around. Still, 'help, help' she shouted. What else was she to
do? Suddenly she heard a man's voice behind her. 'T'what is it at
all and may I be of service to you?' it boomed. Later, all that she
could recall after he had carried her down was the size of his
work-worn hands, and how snuggly they fit under her buttocks.
He felt so right. But what about Desmond, her boyfriend, the
writer, in Dublin?

'The kind of thing that could write itself' is how Declan
described it. Maureen's told him all about the book 'just so he'll
know'. 'Just so I can practise feeling like the eejit I'm going to feel
when it comes out, more like' he has said to me. As much of an
eejit as he feels every time he's out for a splash in his togs and
people stop and point at his belly and ask 'why the black
banana?'.

I think he's depressed. Which is why I'm making the effort to
meet him. The last time we spoke about his 'situation' he
expressed a desire to chuck it all in a single, grand, no-going-back
gesture.

'And what would you do then?' I asked him, 'live on fresh air
and clever couplets?'

'Actually, I was thinking of becoming a travel writer,' he said.

'But I thought you didn't like travelling on your own,' I pointed
out to him.

'But if I was travelling with a *purpose*, if it was my *job*,' was his
answer. 'I loved Asia, in between the feeling weird,' he laughed.

I find it a relief that he can still laugh at himself. He's on the
rocks but still together, I reassure myself on his behalf. The travel
writing idea sounds to me like some form of self-flagellation,

some form of penance for the loss of Maureen. Or maybe it's just running away. And if you're going to run away, why not turn it into a job? See? Logic! He's not going looney. I didn't say that to him, of course, I just said, 'Declan, if that's what you want to do, great, you're clever enough to be the best at whatever you turn your hand to. But don't burn any bridges. Leave your options open, there's no need to annoy anyone.'

Inspired by Breege perhaps, instinct tells me that all he really needs at the moment is a hand to pat him on the back and a voice full of care, going, 'There, there, you're all right.' We might feel like big shots out of our nappies and off in the nasty world, but we all need the proxy mammy sometimes. That's me in this case, I decide.

Declan lovie, wait up, I'm coming.

I arrive in Baggot Street with three minutes to spare for my J'♥ Moi appointment. Time to run across the road and have a quick coffee? My feet have carried me through the traffic despite myself. You could walk blindly into any door along this stretch and chances are you'd end up in a coffee shop, there's that many.

I head into Jitters for my fix.

'Short Americano to go,' I say.

Whatever happened to 'a cup of tea in the hand. And a bun'?

'And a *pain au chocolat.*' Feck it, I've two minutes. I'm starving. I'll wolf it down before I go in. It's probably not etiquette to walk into a beautician's munching pastry. Ideally you've to pretend you never eat, even if your wobbly bod says otherwise.

I climb the stairs to J'♥ Moi.

'Sorry, sorry, sorry Trish, late as usual,' I pant, my takeaway Jitters cup a giveaway.

'You're all right, Mary, I'm running behind schedule myself. Take a seat. Wax isn't it, the lot?'

'No, not bikini, everything else.'

'Grand.'

She shoots off into one of the curtained cubicles. You can hear the gurgle of a facial steam machine. There's a rip, a polite groan and a 'nearly done now' from another cubicle. Everything's hushed here, sweet-smelling and relaxed, to get you in the mood for ladylike torture.

A woman presents her bottom to me from a poster on the wall opposite.

I know I have the perfect bottom, I know you haven't her haughty eyes say, as she stares at me over her brazen shank. Who are you telling? It's like comparing marble and pebble dash. But I'd worry if my whole self esteem was based on my behind. Do I care that much about my bum? I'm not the one looking at it.

'You've a fine arse on ya,' Rory is fond of saying, in his mock-farmer accent. 'I bet you say that to all your lovers,' I rile him. He just laughs. He doesn't care. Neither do I, do I?

I pick up a glossy slab of a magazine and begin flicking. There's another woman waiting in the seat opposite. She's older than me, slim, tall, well dressed, great hair. Her nails are buffed, make-up discrete but perfect, eyebrows exemplary, legs up there with Barbie.

Jaysus, what's she in here for? Just a little knee polish? File my shoulder down a little bit, will you; spray a coat of lacquer over me just to keep me all immaculate? I brush a stray crumb from my jacket, quietly slurp my coffee and flip onto the social pages. I don't buy glossies, but love catching up on who's who, or whoever they think they are:

Opening of the Supper Room at the Harrington Hotel, I read.'*Minimalist, modernist, cosmopolitan with a touch of West of*

Ireland peasant' is how Bohola-born Owen de Maguire describes his personal style: 'Manhattan meets Mayo'. He has magnificently translated his signature in this, his first interior.

Owen is a fashion designer who first hit it big with 'The Wicker Shoe'. Then he did 'The Heather Hat' and there was no stopping him. And then he branched out into cups and saucers, napkins, shelves, doorknobs, that kind of thing. It's de Maguire lifestyle. And now this interior. The magazine describes it as:

Stitched leather sofas redolent of native turf piles, woven hay upholstery, drapes the colour and texture of silage, soda bread loaf cushions with St Brigid's cross buttons.

He is very, very successful, so successful that he's not just a man anymore, he is a CONCEPT – Owen de Maguire is: Connaught Zen. 'And a bit of an idiot,' Monica added when she was explaining all this to me.

Monica heads up the team who do the actual designing; he's too big to do it himself, now that he's been overtaken by the CONCEPT of himself. He just puts his name to whatever the stuff is: Owen de Maguire. In fact, he doesn't *even* have to do that, he just had to sign his name once, and it was turned into the rubber stamp, embroidered label, whatever, that designates it's his. Ten times the price and you're paying into the theory that Owen has sanctioned your choices – 'Hello, fancy a cup of tea in *my* Owen de Maguire cup? Park your arse on *my* Owen de Maguire cover slip and don't even ask what's that scent in the room ...' This is Owen de Maguire living. Inane money meets snappy wrapping, Monica's ideas meet the chic clever-culchie signature.

Now that I think of it, I was actually at The Harrington Hotel Supper Room opening. I scan the pictures to see if I'm in any; I don't remember being snapped. There's Monica, wearing her camera face. She doesn't believe in smiling, she thinks it makes you look eager.

'People think you're a pushover if you're all nicey nicey. Remember, the wheel that squeaks gets the oil,' is one of her mantras.

You can read her philosophy on her face, with her ask-me-I-probably-have-the-answer expression and her Germanic glasses. And you know, she could be right. She looks a lot better than the eejit in the background, laughing and man-handling finger food into her gob. God! Do people not realise when there are photographers around? Oh, hang on. It's me. And the photo is just distinct enough to see there's a bit of sushi hanging off my tooth. Great.

'Ready for you now, Mary,' Trish calls, and not a second too soon.

She shows me to a cubicle, and leaves me to undress. First thing I notice is the cellophane-wrapped paper panties on top of the modesty towel. I leave them aside, by her spatula. No, no intimate waxing, not today. Down to my own humble underwear, I awkwardly pull the towel over me as I clamber on the table. Suitably covered and prone, I breathe into the moment's stillness, before, with a quick open-and-close snap of the cubicle curtains, Trish is back.

'Full wax, is it?' she asks in her sing-song 'I'm efficient and busy, but your friend' voice.

'No, just underarm and leg.' We've already had this conversation, remember. I know where it's leading. I can feel my fanny tense up at the thought.

'Full leg?'

'No, just below the knee.' Do women really get woolly thighs?

'And you're not having the bikini?' She asks, holding the paper knickers in front of my face. Here we go...

I nod in the negative. Best not to bring words into this issue. I'm prostrate now and she's checking the temperature of the pink wax heating in her electric skillet. She's flexing her spatula, she's lining up the cloth strips she'll employ to rip the hair out of me. Trish hates body hair and she's a determined perfectionist. I'm just a hairy blot on her beautician's horizon. She wants the lot of it off at the follicle, and she wants it now. She comes across as obsessive about it, but I suppose that's what makes her good. That's why I am here. Or so I tell myself, to justify being back in this situation.

'No, no, but my toes need doing, I've noticed they're getting hairy. The big ones.' I wiggle them to distract her. They look vulnerable, far away on their own, at the ends of my mottled hairy legs. I feel like a kid.

'No man on the scene?' she inquires cheekily, (reading my underwear?) but not being fobbed off.

'No, no. No one is going anywhere near my bikini line any time soon. You know me, terminally single ...' I give her a bit of generic lady-jabber.

What I'm really saying is 'no one' includes you. Stay away from the pubis, back off from the nether lips and while you're at it take your hands off my butt; it doesn't bother me that there's hair there, so it shouldn't bother you. NO, I am not interested in being left with just a neat little 'landing strip', NO, I'm not interested in the all-off option, NO, I don't care if men find it very sexy/pleasurable/Pamela Anderson/lovely. I just KNOW that the one time you FORCED me into it, Rory's comment was, 'that looks scary' and he put the lights out, and left them out for several weeks until it had all scratchily grown back. As it did, he said it was like there was a man's stubbly chin between my legs, and 'believe it or not, the feeling that Phil Collins' face is your girlfriend's gee is not a turn-on' he said. So NO, I couldn't care less what women do in Brazil or California or Hollywood even. This is Ireland. It is cold here. That is why we are genetically given the big knicker beard and that's good enough reason for me to hang onto it.

She says, 'Well, it's very hygenic. I can have it done in ten minutes, no bother.'

I love that, kinky waxing wrapped up as hygiene! She thinks Irish women are shy, that they really want the whole hog but cannot say it, so she over compensates. She ends up coming across as a depilatory fetishist with an unhealthy bum hair fixation. Why can't I just tell her that? Why can't I just tell her, you know, every woman doesn't want to look like she's ready for an XXX casting. Every woman doesn't equate sexy with the porn-norm. Why can't I just say NO? Instead I say, 'Well, actually, I've got my period at the moment, first day, heavy, know what I mean?'

'OK so.'

That makes her back off. Good. When in doubt, menstruation.

Soon her nose is in my armpit, examining the direction of the hair, slathering the wax on just so, plastering strips over it and ripping them off in vicious jerks. She really, perversely loves this job! When she was a child, did she practise on her cat? 'Fluffy Woofy' when she got given him, 'Kojak' when she was finished.

'Ow, ow, ow,' I say at each tear. Miaow, miaow, miaow.

'Are you OK?'

'Yeah, grand.'

I'm not, it's bloody sore. I try to focus on the Enya cd playing on the PA, but that just adds to the torture. Assaulted on all fronts ...

'Any special reason for the treatment?' Trish chirps in.

'Ermm, I'm on 'Afternoon Stew' this afternoon. Just thought I'd get spruced up.'

'Wearing something revealing?' she asks. The obvious question – why go through this otherwise?

'No, actually, just what I was wearing when I came in. Trousers and jacket.'

'Lovely,' she says, and this line of inquiry grinds to a halt.

Yes, it is illogical. No one will know the secret smoothness of the leg beneath the trousers, no one could guess at the freshly hairless powdered pit of the arm beneath the sleeve. I'll know. I'll know I've made the effort, even if I fail to ignite the *Trash the Pants* chat. It's a trade-off to give me confidence: I want to be smooth, smooth of leg and armpit, if not of chat. And there's also Rory. Later.

'Going anywhere nice on your holidays this year?' Trish asks as she moves in on my shins. I notice she shows no interest in *why* I might be appearing on 'Afternoon Stew'.

'No,' I say, and leave it at that. I don't want the conversation veering back to bikini lines.

For a while there's just the rip of hair and the wails of Enya between us. Hair away, hair away, hair away ...

'Turn over and let me at your calves,' she orders. I mooch over on my belly with all the elegance of a beached whale, clinging to the towel as I manoeuvre. She might reflexively smatter hot wax on my muff if she catches a glimpse.

'Your friend was in the other week,' Trish announces.

I know it's Monica she's talking about. It was she who

introduced me to J'♥ Moi. What was she having done? Do I need to know?

At my first *The Irelander* party a 'real' journalist asked me this question: 'If you're in your friend's house, and she leaves the room, and you notice an open letter on the mantlepiece, is your first instinct to sidle over and have a quick gander at the contents?' Apparently, if the answer is no, then you're not a journalist. My answer was no. Nor did I ever want to creep around TDs' filing cabinets or doorstep The Nutter or The Rachet about drug smuggling and knee cappings or head into the Middle Eastern sunset in a flak jacket, fretful about being kidnapped or killed.

My deepest investigations for *The Irelander* have been into myself: Navelgate. (Not that I can say I'm over the moon that my *raison d'être* these past fourteen months has been letting Ireland know that 'I think what passes for tempura here is a travesty', and 'hey, diets just don't work for me,' and why 'it's cats nil, dogs one as far as I'm concerned'). Maybe I should start being a bit nosier.

'Oh yeah?' I say, leading Trish on. She is the soul of indiscretion.

'She was in an adventurous mood, I sold her my new "Shamrock Tuft". Have I told you about my new stencil waxes?'

'No. The shamrock tuft? Down below, I presume?'

'Of course. I also do The Arrow, The Circle, The Triangle, The Revolver. I've got a portfolio of polaroids, if you'd like to see?'

'No thanks, think I'll give it a miss.'

So Monica is now sporting a hairy shamrock? I didn't think she was the kind of person who'd go for that sort of thing. At all. We've only been friends all of our adult lives and still she's able to surprise me. I feel vaguely miffed about her muff. Trish is making me annoyed at what I don't know about my friend's minge grooming? Jesus, get a grip, I tell myself.

'I could have dyed it green, too, but she wouldn't go for it,' she's telling me now. I can't risk asking her to shut up when she's only halfway through torturing the hair out of me. So I let her go on, 'I do all the primary colour – blues and reds and a bleach, for bleached blondes …' and I ignore her.

I was down in Claredunny with Mammy on Paddy's weekend. I missed all the craic, obviously. Monica and I haven't even had the chance of a proper tête à tête since then. We didn't really get a chance to catch up last night because the cavernous Mart Bar turns into a seething warehouse of din whenever there's a crowd of two or more, and of course we were having one of our narky nights.

I don't know why what Trish is telling me makes me feel insecure. I want my friendship with Monica to be more 'giving', more 'open'. Maybe Monica has different feelings about it. I suppose I get my idea of female friendship from the women's magazines my mother reads:

Then My Friend said 'you can have my kidney!'

Friend gave me sixteen eggs before I gave birth!

'Borrow my husband,' generous friend offered!

The 'Now that's what I call friendship!' school of uncomplicated chums.

'… or stripes if so requested. Now, finito,' Trish declares, primping my legs in a white smog of baby powder.

Just as I'm rising, she grabs a foot and stops me getting up.

'Oh, Jesus, talk about the woolly mammoth, look at your toes! I nearly forgot.'

I'm flattened again, getting my feet perfected.

'She's in again later for a touch-up. That's the thing I will say about the stencil effect – the touch-ups.'

'Tell her I said hi. No, on the other hand don't, Trish, will you? Don't say I was in. I'd hate her to think we were talking about her.'

'Fair enough, I'm schtum, you know me.'

'Yeah. I do. Thanks.'

'Sure about the goggle?' She tries one last time, just before it's all over.

CHAPTER 5

I arrive at Bageluscious before Declan. The lunch rush hasn't
started yet; there's barely a queue. I order a wheat-free, low-fat
cream cheese, guacamole and bacon, and a long cappuccino. I
find a table by the window, and sit waiting for him. I munch,
thinking I should have had the smoked salmon; this bacon
doesn't taste so much cooked as blow-dried. I could have gone
full-fat on the cheese, and it wouldn't have killed me to go 100%
wheat on the bagel either, would it? Why is wheat now one of the
baddies, and what'll be next, apples? Hang on, apples are already
bad, I read somewhere; they *ferment* rather than *digest*, if you
don't watch them.

My cappuccino is lost in the huge cardboard cup. I agitate it to
make sure there's the slosh of something in there. Barely. I seem
to be sucking on nothing but foam. It's hard to tell when and if
I've gone from suds to liquid. Maybe the Polish girl who made it
hasn't been properly trained in on the machine? I'm just wondering if I should bring it back when Declan arrives.

Portly, dishevelled, unshaven – think a chubby Byron in jacket
and jeans. That's Dec. His predominating feature is his mass of
grey-brown curly hair. It blooms out of the open V of his shirt,

creeps along the back of his hands up his fingers. And the more intimate parts of his body you can just imagine. Not that I ever have; ours is not that kind of relationship. Up top the hair acts as a mood compass, increasing in frizz and volume in direct proportion to his level of anxiety. As he walks toward me he looks like he's wearing a fuzzy pyramid on his head.

'Hi, thanks for your PROMPT ATTENDANCE. Your requirements extend to another coffee or anything?' he asks, joining the queue. Bombastic, this is one version of Declan under pressure.

'OK. Cappuccino, and could you specify a liquid one?'

He nods.

I'll know it's really bad if he gets a bun. The muffin test: he's a crisis eater. We learned that when we went to Weightwatchers together.

He comes back with the drinks, his bagel, and a muffin stuck in each pocket.

'There,' he says plonking a coffee in front of me, 'one CAPPO D'CINO, extra wet.'

He sits down and starts into his lunch with an urgency that has little to do with hunger. He doesn't bother taking the muffins out of his pockets.

'You look NICE, Ms McNice,' he declares loudly through a mouthful of bagel sandwich. He's obviously noticed that some of my clothes have had a run-in with an iron. I'm usually completely un-pressed.

'Yeah, think I told you, I'm on telly this afternoon: 'Afternoon Stew'.' I try and talk calmly, slowly, quietly – to bring his tone down.

'So televisionland allows OUR LADY MARY over its hallowed borders again.'

It doesn't work. I go even softer.

'No, not exactly. It's just a one-off. You know, interview thing. I know the producer. She thought I'd be good for the discussion today.'

Which has the opposite effect on Declan, of course.

'As we, who know you, know – YOU WILL.'

I try a normal tone of voice.

'Thanks. Yeah, it's my first time as a commentator, I suppose. It'll hopefully lead to more appearances, you know, reviewing and stuff.'

'Ah, the ONGOING EXIGENCIES of the so-called career of my friend MARY. And what, pray tell, are you commentating on?'

'*Trash the Pants.*'

'TRASH THE PANTS?'

'Yeah.' To distract him, make him laugh, reach him, I pull the book from my hold-everything-handbag, and show him the cover. It features a couple in silhouette walking into the sunset. There's a silhouette dog too, a Labrador, or some such mutt-of-love, galumphing along at their heels. The sky is streaks of implausible, disturbing garish pink. To the designer it obviously means 'romance, romance', to me it says, 'get down, get down, someone has just dropped an A-Bomb behind the horizon'.

'Uggh,' Declan responds.

'Yup. Another self-help manual for the desperate singleton. Summary in a nutshell – wear a skirt and live happily ever after ever. Sample advice: smile, that could be your husband eating an omelette at the next table. Bestseller. American, of course. I'm the Sample Thirty-Something Singleton. That's the little media hole

I've scratched for myself, it seems. God forbid I should ever get married, or worse still, turn forty, I'd be finished.'

'I won't ask you to elope so,' he says.

Good, he's quieter.

'Don't,' I laugh.

'Seriously, dear, do you really think it's a good idea to go on national television pitching yourself as the PROFESSIONAL SPINSTER? It's a bit, errgh ... I dunno.'

'Errgh ... what?'

'SPINST – SPINSTERISH. Exposing. Just protect yourself, that's all. As we ALL must.'

'Oh, that reminds me,' I say, changing the subject. 'My friend Breege – you know my friend Breege? She had a baby boy last night. Malachy. I saw him this morning. Incredible.'

'MALACHY?'

'I know.'

'Ah, BABIES, reminds me of my brilliant *Skittery Ditty* for *Poopy Pants* nappies. Binned, but a dazzler, remembered only by ME. Good copy is hard if you're not prepared to be a plagiarist, I'm always saying. But everyone else is too busy trawling the web and back issues of *Lürzer's Archive* at O'C, O'C, O'D & Y to listen.'

O'C, O'C, O'D & Y is Declan's agency: O'Connell, O'Connor, O'Donnell & Yakamoto.

'OK, what's up? What's wrong?'

'NOTHING. I am just fabadoobie. FAB-A-DOO-BIE.'

'You've a pitch this afternoon, right?'

'*C'est vrai.*'

'And?'

'And, I just need a breather, a bit of human contact. I've been up half the night with my art director ...'

'So, get your head together, go in, and, you know, knock 'em dead. As ever.'

'JUS' LIKE THAT!' he says, doing Tommy Cooper hands.

'So tell me?'

'*COME AND GET IT!*,' Declan more or less shouts. People are looking around at him.

'Shh. For fecks sake, Declan, get a grip,' I lose the rag with him.

In response he just breaks open the second muffin. I was hoping it was for me.

'Do you want to know just how totally, like, FAB-A-DOO-BIE *Come and Get It* is?'

'Stop saying fabadoobie, tell me a mini bit about your pitch, please reassure me you're sane, and then I'm afraid I *have* to go.'

'OK. Fab–a– No. OK. Seriously. IN BRIEF, the brief was to name and create the campaign for the product. First the name, COME AND GET IT! that's mine. Good, yeah? I'll answer: more than good. ASTOUNDING. Then the campaign itself – say COME AND GET IT enough times, in enough winning ways, make the packaging attractive enough and the whole thing will be such a strong call to action, that men – that's who were aiming at – will stop whatever they're doing and head off to COME AND GET IT. Actual ideas: One of the posters has the headline 'FETCH!'. You see a cool guy on all fours with Come and Get It between his teeth. One TV features a good-looking gal, looks like she's seducing a guy; she says 'COME AND GET IT!' and he runs straight past her to the shops to get it. Get the gist? COME AND GET IT, come and get it, come and get it, come and get it, come and get it–'

'I get it,' I cut him off.

'The ultimate product. The ultimate campaign.'

'Mmm, impressive,' I say. 'And what actually *is* Come and Get It?'

'The product itself?'

'Yeah.'

'Chocolate.'

'Chocolate?'

'Yeah. Chunky Man Chocolate, plain milk, and Come And Get It Jawbreaker, with whole nuts and chewy bits ...'

'Right, OK.'

'... of nougat.'

'Well, I don't know much about advertising, but your name and campaign sound brilliant to me. Well done, Declan. I can see why you're wanted.'

'You think it's all a waste. I can tell by the look on your face.'

'No, I do not.'

'You do. You've got your big "isn't 'it amazing what constitutes top dollar work in this day and age" look on your face.'

'I don't.' OK, maybe I do, but I say, 'I think that's coming from you yourself.'

'Maybe it is,' he says, dangerously subdued.

'Please don't go into your pitch in that mood, Declan.'

In reply, he just munches on his muffin.

I was at complete loose end career-wise when I got back from London and I clearly remember this self-same disgruntled man singing me the praises of copywriting at the time.

'Just give it a go,' he told me. And as an encouragement, he lent me his precious copy of *Ogilvy on Advertising*. 'THE Bible' he called it, not really ironically, (the destructive irony has only really set in since the end of Maureen). Well, Mr Ogilvy certainly did well out of advertising. I couldn't get past the bit where he boasted about the length of the hedge he ended up owning around the chateau in France. I've never had big ambitions in the 'owning miles of my very own French hedge' department.

There seemed to be some sort of Faustian trade-off going on; intuitively I said no. I told Declan as much, thanking him for his offer of help and contacts and all that. (I think that's the point that he went from 'nice guy I know' to 'friend', if one were to qualify such things.) I went it alone anyway and I applied for a job in RTÉ instead. But I can see what a great career Declan has made out of copywriting, and, yet again, I tell him as much. For all that he says it's easy, I can tell it's absolutely not – and for all sorts of reasons, not just technical. But he's not in the mood to hear.

'Yes, Mammy,' is all he says.

'Good boy,' I tell him. I'm hoping he'll heed me. I feel like I'm my mother, telling me that law is your only man.

We finish our coffees.

'I'm outta here,' I say, getting up.

'Me too,' he adds, rising at the same time. We accidentally bang heads.

'Declan,' I say, 'watch what you're doing.'

We bear hug each other outside and exchange good lucks before heading off on our separate adventures.

CHAPTER 6

'Taxi, taxi' I yell at the traffic on Baggot Street. I'm just another suit on a street of lunchtime suits now, all of us jostling along about business. Except my business is silly business. Declan has ignited my inner question mark, and now, to be honest, I feel sick at the thought of blathering away on national television: 'Oh yeah, I'm single. What did I think of the book as a single person? What way do I think the singleton vote will swing in the next election? How do singletons feel about the war in Iraq? Are singletons human like the rest of us? There's so many categorically single people now we virtually *are* the rest of us.' I don't want to be known as the voice of 'singletondom'. OK, I'll admit I might have some commitment issues, but I don't want to turn that into a career.

You know, I'd love to be just your bog-standard pundit: just sail through life like a carefree brick.

'RTÉ television centre,' I tell the taxi driver.

'Going on the telly yourself?' the driver asks me. He's been giving me the thrice-over in the rear-view mirror.

I tell him I'm a guest on 'Afternoon Stew'.

'Are you anyone I should know?' he wants to know.

'No,' I reassure him, 'I'm nobody.'

'You look at bit like your one on the cookery programme, what's it her name is again?'

I've been told this before …

'Derbhla Dunphy,' I offer.

'That's the one.'

Derbhla – the Irish Nigella. If Nigella is the voluptuous pin-up Goddess of Vittels, making nooky with fillet of this and that in her gorgeous London home, by comparison Derbhla is a Carrickmacross cross-dresser, hefting up feeds in the cobbled together MDF wonderland of her telly kitchen. Nigella Bites, Derbhla Gobbles.

'Thanks. Are you telling me I look like a horse?'

'A lovely horse, ha, ha. No I am not. I wouldn't mind giving her one. '

'I feel better so,' I say, not to let him think he's offended me. Even though he's just half suggested, by deduction, that he'd like to 'give me one', and that's meant to be a compliment. There's nothing like a man with a face like a collapsed airbag fancying you (by default) to take the wind out of your 'I'm fab' sails. Which reminds me – I forgot to phone Mammy to tell her I was on. She'll hear about it at Mass and then I'll never hear the end of it.

'Theresa saw you on 'Afternoon Stew'.'

'Oh, and?'

'And? Why didn't I know?'

'Oh, it was nothing.'

'You never phone.

'I do.'

'You never think about me.'

'Sorry, who is this I'm talking to again?' I'll joke then.

And then she'll hang up.

And when I call back she'll be sniffling.

'Who'd have ever thought I'd be completely off your radar,' she'll say, coming out with the incongruous tellyism.

As if, as the only daughter, my only mother wasn't blinking in the middle of my ruddy radar every day. Her on her own in Claredunny; growing ever older; television her window on the terrifying world; feet firmly planted in other people's business; gaze solidly directed to the past. Poor Mammy, Cormac's always saying. It's easy for him to relate to her with unadulterated pity, seeing as he's doing so from the happy distance of Amsterdam. But personally, being here in Ireland, I'd rather not be tied in knots of Mammy guilt and commiseration. I'd rather it be a woman -to-woman thing. I tried to explain that to Mammy once, when I was younger, and believed in the power of chat.

I can't remember how we got onto it, but I was just back from another island-hopping holiday, and I'd gone down for the weekend before starting back to work. My deep Greek tan must have been making me feel invincible. Either that or the sun had fried my brains.

'I just feel like you don't know me, Mammy,' I said, going for honest.

'But of course I know you, lovie,' she'd said. 'I'm your mother. I know you better than you know yourself. I remember as a baby, you were so quiet. Have I ever told you that? Not a squeak out of you, you never cried. Not a bit like Cormac. Not a squeak. We thought there was something wrong with you.'

'Jesus Christ, there you go again. There you go … I'm a quarter of a century out of nappies, but you still treat me like a baby. Hello? Stuff has gone on with me since then. I've been to college, travelled all over the world, had jobs, had lovers, relationships, done things you wouldn't have ever dreamed of doing. Don't you want to know who this person is?' I was gesticulating like something out of 'The Sopranos' by this stage.

'Your father would be turning in his grave if he could hear you, it's not me you should be confessing this to, you know.'

'I'm not confessing anything, I'm just trying to let you in on my life.'

'I'm not sure I want to know.'

'There, you said it, you just don't want to know. You don't want to know. You think you can phone me up all the time telling me what I should be doing – should have, could have, that's all I get from you. But you don't want to know the facts.'

'What facts?'

'That maybe I am separate and different to you.'

'Stop shouting.'

'I am not shouting,' I shouted, 'I'm just sick and tired of our dysfunctional relationship.'

'I suppose you got that word from Monica, did you? There was no ... dit, whatever you said, no functional relationships in my day. We just had respect.' *Wheeze, wheeze, wheeze* 'Where's my inhaler?'

She had a convenient asthma attack, and, watching her hunched on the couch sucking up her medication, I couldn't help but feel like a petulant kid.

'I'm sorry, Mam,' I said, when she was breathing almost normally again.

'I know, lovie, I know you didn't mean what you said. I know you're a good girl.'

But I did, I did, I did, I did, I did, I said, in my head.

Once, a counsellor (yes, I've paid to chat about why my relationship with my Mammy isn't up there at the level of Daniel

O'Donnell's with his. Eight weeks, €400 to conclude, 'I'm OK, you're OK' and maybe it's Daniel who has the issues and not me) made a pile of cushions on the floor in her office.

'I want you to imagine that that is your mother,' she ordered.

Mother=cushions. Cushions= mother. Mother, cushions.

'Now, jump up and down on them and shout, "I am me" for as long and as loud as you can,' she said, 'you may find this difficult, but try ...'

'OK, you can stop now,' she was yelling at me after fifteen minutes.

'How was that for you?' she asked when we were seated again.

I could only nod, give her the thumbs-up and whisper 'transcendental'. My voice was wrecked.

I'm rummaging through the black hole of my bag, looking for my phone as my head fizzes with all this, and by the time I've dialled and she's answered I'm irritated at the memory of past conversations.

'Hi, Mam?'

'Mary, hello, how are you, lovely to—'

'Just a quick call to let you know I'll be on telly this afternoon.'

'What time?'

'Sometime between two thirty and three, 'Afternoon Stew'.'

'Oh, you're on with Ronan? He's lovely, he has lovely hair, I always think. Although you'd wonder what's under it sometimes. The other day the chef was saying he was going to reduce his sauce, and Ronan says, "what you mean is you're going to take some out of the pan?" Can you believe it? You know, you could do that job in your sleep, instead of ... but I'll say nothing. Sorry, anyway, I won't be in, there's a meeting of The Committee. What a shame. Good luck. Say hello to Ronan for me.'

'Actually, I think it's Martina I'll be talking to ... '

'Her? Oh. What are you discussing?'

'Ermm. A book.'

'Well, better than yesterday. Do you know what she was talking about yesterday? You'd never guess–'

'Twink?' I say the first thing that comes into my head, but her question wasn't seeking an answer, of course.

'–tampoons! On afternoon television, can you believe it?' Apparently they can kill you if you're not careful, but do they have to rub our noses in it at two in the afternoon? Tampoons this, tampoon that, I ask you? Tampoons?'

Obviously they hadn't said the word 'tampon' quite often enough for her to get the pronunciation right.

'Well, rest assured the book I'm discussing is not about tam*poons,*' I tell her, wondering does the word-mangling go in the other direction: harp*ons,* bab*ons,* Vidal Sass*on?* Luckily, she doesn't ask what the book is about. She's the last person in the world who'd want to see me flaunting my lack of a husband and babies on television. It would almost be as bad as me going on and talking about being the only daughter of a widowed mother whose only son is gay, and we all know it, but the mammy will never say it. We just gather around the Christmas table in Claredunny like one big happy family – me beside the empty chair of my ever-absentee-fella, and Cormac with his ever 'Bachelor-Friend', Flavio. And not the squeak of a baby between any of us. But as I'm the owner of the only viable womb, I can't help but feel the weight of the onus. Oh God, what if I were to let some of that slip on television; mad things can happen in front of the camera ...

'Well, best of luck,' Mammy says.

'Thank you.'

'Good girl.'

'OK. Bye.'

We're at RTÉ. I pay and get out, and enter the all-too-familiar foyer. Eamon Andrews is still on the left, in extra-life-size bronze: the first superman of Irish television. You can just hear him going 'England Ahoy' in his sculpted head. On the right the proud display of corporate heirlooms, like a country wife's cabinet of wedding present delph and good crystal. All the recent TV awards are in there, (most circa 1974, it always seems to me).

'Hello, I'm here for ...' I begin and the receptionist waves me to shut-up while she finishes her call.

'... and then just mash the avocado with a fork, add the garlic, drop of olive oil, pinch of salt, black pepper if you like. And don't forget a good squeeze of lemon juice; it'll stop it going black. You're welcome. Tortilla chips, yeah. Any. You're welcome. Bye. See you later.'

She glances at me, 'Yes?'

'I'm here for Clodagh, 'Afternoon Stew'.'

She punches in the researcher's extension number like she's reached the tedium limit and is about to have a massive monotony reaction. I can just see the headlines – Boredom rocks foundations of State Broadcaster! Many feared alive!

'Clodagh, guest at reception,' she drones into her mouthpiece.

I keep my head down and shuffle into the corner, waiting for Clodagh to arrive and whisk me up to make-up. It would be just my luck to bump into Attracta Butt, my last boss, my ticket out of here, an acrimonious departure. If there's one thing that woman has a talent for it's holding a grudge: *Forgive and remember*, that's her motto, without the first bit.

I'm keeping inconspicuous, eyeing passers-by in the cabinet mirrors, pretending to be really interested in a twisted bit of metal that appears to have been awarded to RTÉ by the Belgian Electricity Board, when suddenly I'm knocked back by a wall of bilingual blather.

'Hi, Mary, Mary McNice, nice to see you, to see you nice. What are you doing in these parts? Haven't seen you around in an age. Thought you'd got ye to a nunnery – jesting of course. You're looking *go h-álainn*, love the new hair. Been reading your column; not settled, not breeding, playing the field. God, I admire your honesty in this tiny town; you've some neck. I always said that about you, didn't I? So what brings you out to the centre of the universe? Agus *conas atá an cailín? An bhfuil tú go maith?* Ya ride.'

I can't compose myself in time to sidestep the inevitable slobber on the cheek. I'm now pinned in the corner, face just tongued, flushed with unease. And I know he'll be thinking I'm blushing with latent passion. 'Lady, you've creamed your pants!' That's one of his radio catchphrases, however he gets away with it. 'Finian, hi. As up as ever,' I stutter.

It's Finian Burke, a one-night notch on the bedpost, a notch too far. Oh God, when I think of it, not that I want to. We used to work together, we were off on an over-nighter, staying in some anonymous lodge near roadworks, too much to drink, ended up in the same bed. Morto the next morning: Me, not him.

'And to what do we owe the honour of your presence?'

"Afternoon Stew',' is all I can get out between praying for

Clodagh to appear quick-sharp. I would never have left a guest waiting this long in reception when I was a researcher.

'Oh, umm,' he says.

To deflect any noseying on his part, I say, 'Saw the pic of you tying the knot in the back of *The Sunday Tittler*, congrats, congrats.'

'Oh thanks, that was an age ago. There's a nipper in the mix now.'

'Congrats, congrats'. *Think of some other words, for Christ's sake!* 'God, you're really flying these days ... ' bolster him up a bit and hopefully the helium of his ego will simply float him away.

'Ah, well now ...' he begins.

Whenever Mam sees Finian on television, she says, 'Oh, Mary, there's your friend, he's done very well for himself, hasn't he?' The little all-in-one recognition and dig. Mam thinks I can't catch a glimpse of him on television without comparing our relative careers, seeing as I've know him since I was a researcher, and then the killer – *he's the same age as you, Mary, isn't he?* Yeah, Mam, well maybe for some people the twenties 'what am I doing with my life' angst continues into their forties. So what? Who cares? I'll probably still be feeling it's all to play for when I'm on my death bed.

I should tell Mam sometime that actually I can't see Finian on television without the words '*an bhfuil cead agam* come on your tits' popping into my head.

We're now face to face, a nose between us. Personal space is not his strong suit. I can't help noticing that his skin has that sort of expensive look about it; he must get regular micro-dermo-blasting, or whatever it is you call that treatment. And his smile shines like a new toilet. He has that kind of sheen only spare loola can buy. He's been the presenter of the Saturday prime-time 'Bibbity Bobbity Show' for the last six years; he has his morning radio show, 'Cockadoodledo Dublin'; he's always snipping ribbons at some new supermarket or clinic round the country and in the last year alone he's also done 'Price my Hacienda!' and 'Celebrity Colon!' both produced by his own company, ! Productions, however he swung that one.

He's now telling me about the new travel show he's developing, provisionally titled 'Lads Off Yonder', exclamation point: 'The idea is that you take a gang of four bog-standard lads and each week they're off to a different mystery destination, say like Montserrat. Did you know it's the only place in the world, besides Ireland, that celebrates St Patrick's Day as a national holiday? The idea is to have The Lads' take on the place, you know, like what's The Vatican City got for The Lads, or from The Lads' perspective is Venice all it's cracked up to be? *An dtuigeann tú?* They don't pretend to be into anything other than the beer *agus* the craic *agus* chasing the *gúnas*, gettit? And if the art and shit tickles them along the way, all the better.'

'Thicks on tour?' I suggest.

'*Sin a bhfuil, ya cailín glic* ya.'

Clodagh appears – with apologies for keeping me waiting.

Finian has a point he wants to make: 'Anyway, Mary, what I was going to say was we may need a dig out on the research front, so if you're still in the market give us a bell. Could be some travel involved,' he adds the last bit with a wink and a glint of pristine fang. 'You were good, as far as I can remember,' he says, 'my door's always ajar where you are concerned, know what I'm saying?' And he shoves his card in my breast pocket, allowing his knuckles a good nudge of boob. Nothing changes.

He gives Clodagh a flirty wink and parades off like the cock-king of the hen house.

'Jaysus,' Clodagh lets slip.

'We used to work together, he's all right,' I say, automatically defending him. Why? You have to admire his determination, his energy, his go-gettit positivity. Don't you? OK, I'll come clean with myself. I'm defensive because we slept together, so he can't be *that* bad, can he? Or what does that make me? He asked me out on a date after the Ibis Incident. Give him a chance, I thought, why not, you're hardly killed for choice. He wore a t-shirt that said 'I'm with sexpot', flirted with the barmaid all night and then suggested we invite her back to his place, for a threesome.

I said, 'well good luck with the third party, good night.' I walked home, half crying, half in wonder that I could so need a bit of man/love action in my life I'd ended up out with that scrotum-brain. And kicking myself that I couldn't come up with a much cleverer comeback when he suggested the threesome: 'I would have thought you could have made a threesome with yourself, seeing as you think you're God; or, changing tack, 'what, do you find there's safety in numbers?' Anyway, it's all history now.

Clodagh gives me a for-feck's-sake look as she swipes us through the security door. She pushes it open with her skinny hip and I follow her through. *Hips are the new breasts* – I did two and a half thousand words on that for an in-flight magazine recently.

'OK, he is a bit full of himself,' I admit.

We share a laugh as I follow her along the corridor of dressing rooms, passing a massive portrait of The Man Himself, Finian – this man my mother holds up to me – he's holding hands with Barney™.

'I'll just bring you to make-up first, then you can wait here in the green room,' she gestures to a room on the left, where three dolled-up women in wheelchairs are having coffee. I follow her to the right, up the stairs.

'I think Steve is down to do you,' she says, 'and Kian is already in.'

'Sorry, who did you say?' I ask the back of her head, a prickle of unease attacking my central nervous system.

'Kian, Kian O'Kelly from *The Dublin Evening News*,' she says as she powers on.

We've arrived in make-up. I'm stunned; she's in a hurry.

'Sorry, I wasn't told ... ' I begin to say.

'Yes?'

'... that it was going to be a panel discussion, that there was going to be two of us. I thought it was just me.'

'Oh. No, no. Don't know where you got that idea.' She looks at her clipboard.

'I have it down here. *Trash the Pants*, Kian O'Kelly for, Mary McNice against.'

Sorry about that,' she singsongs and she's gone. Not as sorry as me ...

CHAPTER 7

'Hello Mary, lovely to see you. Sit up there and I'll see if I can plaster your cracks,' Steve invites me to his leather swivel make-up throne. I know him from working in here. We always had a good laugh together, but I'm not exactly laughing now as 1) I absorb the information Clodagh has just slapped in my face, and 2) I notice my Arch Nemesis being powdered three seats away from me.

'Shit-it-ee-doo-daa, I've forgotten my polyfilla,' Steve quips as I swaddle myself in a gown and plonk myself down at his mercy.

'Just give me the standard bag-on-the-head then,' I pick up his tone and banter, trying to hide my quiet panic. No one mentioned I was debating with anyone, with a man, with Kian I've-Got-An-Opinion-And-You-Don't-Exist-O'Kelly. I feel like I've been set up. This is just wonderful: I'll be woman, declaring my trousers are attractive to men, and Kian will be man, saying no, no they're not – i.e. no, *you're* not. Attractive. To. Men. And I'm man so let me be the judge of that. Hag-features. He'll probably base his whole column on it tomorrow: Too Much a Boot for Love, or Husband Where art Thou, Bemoans She-Man; I could write the headline myself.

Kian is not so much a hack as a thug. 'Dublin bites Back' is his by-line. It's all: '*We* don't agree with this, *we* hate the way that, such and such is a talentless gnat and don't *we* know it.' Am I the *only* one who ever wonders where he got his royal 'we' license? He's crowned himself King of Snide. The 'we' is himself and his arse and he's made a career out of talking through it.

And I'd say good luck to him, if I myself hadn't been the butt of his pen. He attacked me with his ink when I was fired over my 'View from Behind'/'TellyBelly' column. I can still see it in my head when I close my eyes and think 'worse thing that ever happened to me':

NOT NICE MARY

MYSTERY COLUMNIST MYSTERY NO MORE.
A K. O'K. exclusive.

DUMPED

Anonymous spill-the-beans RTÉ insider has been unceremoniously dumped. TellyBelly, whose 'comedy' column in *another paper* poked 'fun' at life within the national broadcaster, has been unmasked. She is lowly researcher Mary McNice, 29. AND SHE'S OUT ON HER EAR.

CRAP

Mary, whose crap sketches involved thinly disguised RTÉ personalities, had been indulged by the powers-that-be UNTIL NOW. They have finally woken up to the small matter of BREACH OF CONFIDENTIALITY.

NOT GAS

Her pathetic catchphrase, 'it's gas, isn't it!' might have let her get away with it BEFORE. But YESTERDAY she was given a resounding 'not gas' and her contract was TERMINATED with immediate effect.

STUPID

A little bird tells me the final straw came when a character called THE POISON DWARF appeared in her column. Those in the know were SHOCKED by the similarity between THE DWARF and Mary's boss, series producer ATTRACTA BUTT. Now that's what we call stupid. Nice work, Mary McNice. At least you know the DIPLOMATIC SERVICE won't be coming knocking for your CV.

DEAD END

But don't worry, Mary, even though most media employers wouldn't touch you with a BARGE POLE after this, we're sure you'll have no bother finding a new home for your researcher 'talents' elsewhere. Call centres are always looking for people to man the phones. You'll even be able to get a new 'column' out of it: Dead End Job Mary. But this time THE JOKE WILL BE ON YOU.

NOT FUNNY

We say good riddance. 'The View From Behind' won't be missed. Let's face it: IT WAS AS FUNNY AS A FOUR YEAR- OLD'S FUNERAL.

When Monica read his piece, she phoned up and said I should look on the bright side.

'What bright side?' I asked.

'He got your age wrong! He's promoting you as still twenty-something. I'd have that bit made into a t-shirt for the week-end.'

She took me out that night to toast my notoriety in Chumps, our favourite restaurant. ('Let me pay, you're financially fucked now!!!'

she joked when we'd finished our three-bottle-of-nice-wine din dins.) Derek, the debonair maitre'd, said he should be asking for my 10x 8 to put on the wall. Oh, how we all laughed! It made it almost seem all right on the night. But, in truth, the experience devastated me. Yeah, maybe I was naïve, and stupid and not funny and not gas and crap and EVERYTHING he said, but losing my job was punishment enough. I'd just applied for the directors/producers course and there was no way I'd be considered after that. No maybes about it. I was thoroughly stupid. But having Kian O'Kelly script my stupidity like that, and for it to be in one of the most widely read newspapers in the country? That really took the biscuit. It was like being stripped in public and put in stocks for everyone to sling mud at you. It was devastating. I was in bits. I got home, crawled under my duvet and cried until the next evening.

Then Rory came round with chocolates, champagne and a greenhouse of lilies, and said, and I quote, 'all you do is you put a spin on it'.

'What do you mean by that?' I asked him, after we downed the not one, but two, bottles of bubbly.

'Basic law of The Science of Rory Publicity,' he answered, 'in direct proportion to how awful something may seem, the equal and opposite may also be made to be true.'

'Don't talk shite,' I said.

'I can't help it, it's my job,' he replied.

'You're drunk,' I said.

'And that's what makes me so good,' he said.

Rory is a publicist for a massive promoter. He's great at his job and he's got clout – call it connection to hundreds of thousands of euro worth of annual press advertising. He also has an enhanced sense of what's do-able, as you might have if you have an Access All Areas attitude to life: The whole 'TellyBelly' idea was his in the first place; he nursemaided me through the process of getting the commission. 'I'm here to Mollycoddle you, don't worry,' he laughed, when Molly Finnegan said yes to a trial commission. I suppose it helped that he knew her; she was a close friend of his family's.

So, after the firing, which obviously left me high and dry as 'TellyBelly', I took Rory's advice. I met with Molly Finnegan, told her that now 'Tellybelly' was finished I wanted something bigger and better under my own name. (I'd rehearsed all this with Rory beforehand, he told me precisely what I wanted.) I surprised myself with how convincing I was.

She said, 'yes, fine, you've got your column, page three, a thousand words.' We agreed on the title 'Attitude' and that was that. I know sisters are supposed to be doing it for themselves all the time now – but sometimes all you need is the feeling that there's someone standing behind you, or indeed standing shoulder to shoulder with you, in a personal capacity: a formally undefined capacity perhaps, but personal nonetheless. Rory was there for me.

He also helped me break into the fringes of freelance – suggested my first piece: 'Celebrity Molars', 5000 words, €50, *The Leinster Orthodontist*. Like he said I would, I have been steadily building on that one cent a word start since.

That was fourteen months ago: Let's have the DA, DA, DA, DA soundtrack now, and the man who hands me the book and says 'MARY McNICE, THIS IS YOUR LIFE.' Did you ever wonder how it would be if you got so famous someone decided to do a 'This is Your Life' on you? Wouldn't you be afraid it'd just be a sequence of one mortally embarrassing episode after another? Peppered with people you'd hoped never to set eyes on again?

'What look are we going for?' Steve asks jokily as he pulls the hair back from my face.

'Oh, just general fabulousness,' I say, feigning afternoon telly cheer.

'My speciality,' says Steve.

'I know,' I tweet back at him.

Steve covers a sponge in Mac and starts dabbling my face. I watch the pair of us in the mirror: him streaked in fake tan as ever, trim in his tight 'Will Golf for Food' t-shirt, engrossed in his task despite the chitchat. I try to think about things other than my past history in this place. I am required to be up, back in RTÉ for the first time since my down-  fall, facing the journalist who rubbed my nose in it. And on live television. All I can do now is handle it like the professional I'm not. Just fake it 'til it's true, baby! Who said that? Emperor Charlie?

So I focus on Steve's t-shirt, maybe there's an 'Attitude' in it: 'Will Golf for Food? Is 'Golf' a euphemism for some daring new Dublin sex act? Whack my balls, birdie and give me a handicap? Who knows what your modern Irish homosexual is up to these days. Is there a gay golf scene? How does gay golf differ from straight golf; florals instead of checks?

Or is the reference to golf post-ironic irony? How can you know, when everything skitters around on the high stilts of 'kno-wingness' these days? I don't know. How can you know what's what now?

I'm reminded of Miriam's 'What's Then/What's Now' column in *Midweek*, idea nicked from a zillion similar What's In/What's Out, Up/Down, Over/Back, Old/New, Right/Wrong, Brown/Black, Stop/Go, ↑/↓, You're a Troglodyte/No You're Not print fillers elsewhere, everywhere. Jesus, if the readers could only see the people who are telling them what's hot 'n' not! What's this Miriam came up with in the last one: Biscotti were THEN, and, on a retro up-swing, re-issued Jacob's Chocolate Gold Grain were NOW.

Maybe Steve's t-shirt is just plain literal: Will golf for food? Maybe he would rather earn a living as a subsistence golfer.

'Hello, calling occupants of inter-planetary most extraordinary Mary head,' Steve bleats.

'Oh, sorry, I was off with the fairies there for a minute,' I say.

'Ha, ha. Stop or I'll laugh my wings off.'

'Sorry.'

'There was me thinking that now because it's you and not someone you've researched sitting in the pampering seat, I was getting the cold shoulder. Now that you're a newspaper celebrity and all.'

'Well, if I'm a celebrity, I must say I'm finding the anonymity of it thrilling.'

'I love your column. Is it all true? Is that really your life and your take on things, or is it made up for the billies?'

'What do you think, Steve?' I ask him.

Out of the corner of my eye I'm watching Kian in his mirror, studiously ignoring me. Why didn't I just say a polite hello when I came in? Dublin is just too small to have ongoing agendas with people. I should have been bigger than the fact that he ripped me to shreds in print. Now we're into the official 'we don't say hello to each other' zone. It makes me uncomfortable.

'Dunno,' Steve responds. 'For instance, are you really terminally single, or is that just for your editor and in real life there's a six foot-something stud in bulging jocks making the cheese on toast when you get home in the evening?'

'Your fantasy, not mine, methinks,' I answer.

I'm no good at lying. If I was, I'd be saying, loudly, for Kian's benefit, since I'm here as the fall guy, the 'media singleton': 'Well, Steve, you'll never guess. Three months ago in Dunnes, reaching for the last courgette, another hand gets there first – male, manly, ringless. A "you have it", "no, you have it" battle of vegetable generosity begins, and ends as the green lozenges of my eyes dissolved in the blue pools of his. I went home with the courgette and his phone number. Setanta is his name, he's a Ryanair pilot (good but not that good, keep it real) and I'm not saying it's a textbook case of love at first sight and happy every after, but ...' But I am no good at lying.

'What about your love life? I always found that a lot more interesting than anything I could muster,' I deflect the question.

'I was dating a clairvoyant but he didn't see a future in it,' he answers.

'Hilarious,' I say. 'Did you make that one up yourself, or get it from the head joke-writer in here?'

'I'm serious. I was, it's true.'

I glance at his face, and can see the truth of it in his expression. Sometimes it must be hard being Steve; conversation to him is just a batting back and forth of fripperies. But what when the whimsy rating is zero? Imagine Steve telling his mates that he has cancer? Yippee. Let's go wig shopping, they'd probably say. He's confused the noun and the adjective of being gay; definitely not

Cormac's cup of tea. But Steve's good humour is his subconscious armour. I respect that.

'Oh, I'm sorry,' I say.

'I will survive,' he retorts.

Kian gets up and exits without acknowledging me. I take a deep breath.

'Are you guys on together?' Steve asks when Kian is well out of earshot.

'Yeah, unfortunately. Not looking forward.'

'Brave lady, you go, girl. And what, may I ask, are you talking about?'

'Well, apparently we'll be discussing whether or not Kian finds me attractive.'

'Come again,' Steve says, puzzled.

'We're talking about this derivative piece of shite excuse for a book called *Trash the Pants* in which an American chick, a Dr Chick, what else, says, "put on the slap and a frock, turn yourself into your own dowry and bag a moneybags for a happy ever after".'

'I take it you loved it,' he laughs.

'It's my bible now, baby, can't you tell?' I say, swinging round in the chair, arms outstretched. 'You get the picture – Kian will say how right she is, how wrong the likes of drab old me are, and seeing as he has already famously decided to detest me, I'm in for an unpleasant ten minutes in front of the camera.'

'In that case, babe, we're not just going for fabulous. We're going for Supra-Fabulous,' he declares, and he's reached for the glitter-shadow before I can say, 'There's no place like home'.

'I thought you said big hair; obese would've been more accurate,' I tell Steve fifteen minutes later as I take in the fuzzy halo around my painted face.

'It's fabulous, believe me, toots,' he answers, patting, lifting, admiring its lacquered crust. You can almost hear it crunch under his fingers. 'It brings out the real you.'

Since when was I Brian May?

'Thanks a mil,' I say.

Clodagh appears at the door. 'Nearly ready, Mary? We need you downstairs.'

'Remember, you don't get a second chance to make a first impression. Adios,' Steve waves me off.

'I just twigged, you know who it is you really remind me of?' Clodagh offers on the way down.

'Who?' I ask, a smidgen hopefully. Someone good, please.

'Yer one off the cookery programme: Derbhla … Derbhla …'

'Derbhla Dunphy, oh really?'

'Have you got that before?'

'Mmm,' I manage to squeeze out between my glossy lips.

We enter the Green Room. Kian is in the corner, on his mobile. Ignore, ignore, ignore. I sit beside the wheelchair ladies and engage them in banter. They coo over the job that has just been done to my head. 'Ohh,' they all go, in the way women are supposed to respond when one of their sex has made a far-out cosmetic effort. 'It's amazing how glittery blue eyeshadow sets off green eyes,' says the one whose legs were crushed under a Massey Ferguson, 'I'd never have thought of that myself.'

Now that the time is near, I'm nervous. My mother's voice speaks to me:

You know television puts pounds on you – six – twelve – fourteen – I think it is. It's a well-known fact.

Calm down, I tell myself. Nobody watches daytime telly. Do

they? Think of something else … Rory. I first met Rory in this very room. I was a researcher on a show called 'Teen Wow!', and he'd come in with a band I'd booked. Rory is gorgeous – six foot four, a magazine-build, thick hair with a slight cow's lick all over. He made me literally go weak at the knees. Literally go, 'wow' and have to cover it up by going, 'as in "Teen Wow", isn't that the show you're in for, Sebastian?' 'I'm not Sebastian,' he said, 'Rory's the name.' That was the first conversation we ever had.

'*Trash the Pants*,' Clodagh calls. We're on.

Down in the studio, Kian and I are seated either side of Martina, the presenter who will interview us. Kian is flicking through the book, trying to look sharp, which in his case translates as resting your chin in the fat of your neck while you tense the thin slit of your lips: Desperate Dan transmogrified into a flaccid hack. I'm just trying my damnedest not to sink into the over-soft sofa and become Mary Five Bellies, while Martina is staring nervously into the open maw of her autocue camera, waiting for the floor manager to signal the cut to her.

There's that peculiar, intense soundproofed atmosphere you get in television studios: all the behind-camera activity; all the background producing, the budgeting, research and planning; all the personnel, from the runners, boom operators and camera people up to the director and her assistants in the control box; all that equipment and technology; all the sheer expense and effort of it, now focused through the lens and onto the television performer. Martina is riddled with awareness of every nuance of this, when she should be oblivious. You can see it. She's too nervy to be good; our little chat could swing in any direction, because her main concern won't be debate, it'll be to keep anyone's lips moving for ten minutes.

The galaxy of blaring lamps strung from the high overhead rigging make it hot. Plus there's a heady whiff of fish: Pat the telly chef is demonstrating his Zero-Cream Chowder to Ronan. Ronan is the other end of Martina, so relaxed in front of the cameras that he often looks as if he's about to keel over into a snooze in the middle of one of his 'chats'.

'There, have a taste of it yourself,' cook entreats him.

They're behind us in the pretendy kitchen. We hear a manly slurp, a smack of the lips and a drawled 'delicious, and you know, Pat, I wouldn't miss the cream at all. And neither would my belly.' Ronan does his famous laugh: 'Har. Har. Har. Har.' A telly reviewer once described him as a hyena on Lithium.

I can see from a monitor that a camera is swinging round to side pan over us. There's me, about to be beamed nationwide. What am I here for again? My mind draws a blank as the floor manager signals *five, four, three, two, one* under the lens of the autocue. And blast off!

Martina's hands strangle each other in her lap. She's as relaxed as a chimp in a test rocket.

'Women have become TOO assertive, TOO bullish, and SO like men they've stolen the role of the male and made them feel like sissies,' Martina reads intensely from the autocue. If you were sitting at home watching her, you'd think she had some subtext she was trying to signal to you, something like: They've got me against my will. Help! Send bananas …

'… like the woman who pops testosterone pills to win in the boardroom,' she reads, 'but just ends up with the hairy bust, the net effect is to make these women deeply unattractive to the men they ultimately wish to attract.' So says Dr Suzy Wurlerwitz in her new book, *Trash the Pants*. It's been a bestseller in the States, and has just been published here. In the studio with me I have contro-versial journalist Kian O'Kelly, and confessional columnist Mary McNice, and I'm wondering, does Dr Wurlerwitz have a point?'

Confessional? Moi? Bless me, Martina, for I have sinned. Please, not me first. Please, I plead with my eyes.

'Mary.'

Thanks!

'If I may begin by just quoting from a recent column of yours, you say, "seriously, it can't be all my fault I'm terminally single". Whose fault is it then? Men's?'

'Ermm,' I begin, 'I think I was being facetious there, actually. I don't think it's useful to assign blame as such in such things, and I wouldn't agree with the diagnosis of Dr Wurlerwitz …

I pause for one millisecond to recover from the question and get the image of Martina as a chimp out of my head, and straight - away Kian gets his sword out, metaphorically.

'Facetiousness, the last refuge of the desperate …' (What does that mean?) 'The fact is that all these women in their thirties may have wanted a partner, a man, but made no concessions to actu-ally attracting the male of the species, and now they're all going "oh oh, boo hoo, we're left on the shelf" Hilarious. Frankly.'

The 'these women' in that diatribe is plainly me. I feel I'm on trial here, and it's my column that has landed me in the dock. I try to deflect.

'Do people even seriously use that phrase anymore, "left on the shelf"? As if women have a sell-by-date. What about single men? Why don't we talk about men being left on the shelf? Why aren't books been written about that?'

'And what weren't they doing to attract a man?' Martina ignores my point and asks Kian. She very publicly married one of those nouveau Celtic Big Cats last year. Half an issue of *Ceart Go Leor* magazine was devoted to their nuptials – the something-or-other themed tent, the who's-who-who-were-there, and the somebody's-yacht they honeymooned on. Martina is full of knowing ignorance as she appeals to the also married Kian to enlighten her about these single eejits.

And I'm the only 'single eejit' in the 'debate'. I'm the pathetic example. Jesus! I'm simultaneously seething and sinking into the sofa. People watching at home will be thinking 'so that's yer one who writes the column in the paper. So she really is a spinster.'

Kian goes off on one of his famous rants: Men want women who are feminine, naturally. Women want to be feminine, it's nature. Men don't want to be bossed around, cuckolded and made to feel useless. Men are naturally protectors, decision-makers and all round hairy-chesters. They marry the women who allow them to be just that. Dr Suzy Wurlerwitz is absolutely right. In return, the Mrs gets shelves put up, heavy lifting done, and her personal bodyguard to set on any intruders. And all the leftover lonely macho-birds who've realized it's too late to put on a nice frock and make the effort? Maybe they should turn to each other and explore the lesbian option. It's just about all that's open to them by this stage, and they wouldn't even have to be arsed getting out of the dungarees.

Yup, this is the famed Kian edge: a glorified taxi-driver take on the world. And it would be hilarious if it wasn't all directed at me, which in the next millisecond it is:

'Ha, ha, ha, have you ever considered that yourself, Mary?' laughs Martina.

'What, putting on a frilly frock and coming over all baby-voiced?' I quiz.

'No, exploring the lesbian option.'

What? How much more personal is this interview going to get? Is this what I signed up for?

'I don't think it's actually the kind of thing you try on for size, Martina, and, just to refer back to the book we're talking about, I think *Trash the Pants* and all the other recent offerings of its ilk are an insult to women's intelligence. They represent a backlash against hard-won female autonomy, and a reactionary spin on the way society is changing regardless, but yet again it's a case of woman blame thyself ...'

'Well, would you listen to Andrea Dworkin,' Kian pipes.

'She died a while ago didn't she?' asks Martina, following her stream-of-consciousness interviewing technique.

'Yes, died as she lived, in out-sized dungarees, I believe,' he guffaws.

Martina guffaws too. The floor manager indicates for Martina to wrap up.

'That's *Trash the Pants – Re-feminize yourself and find Love,* by Dr Suzy Wurlerwitz, published by Leghorn & Brahmas and on sale now. Last word, Kian?'

'I thought there was a lot of truth in there myself.'

'And Mary, your final thoughts?'

'Obnoxious rubbish.'

'So Kian loved it, Mary hated it. But if you're anything like the single ladies Suzy Wurlerwitz describes in the book, you may find a ring of truth in it. And who knows, if you take her advice you might even find a ring on your finger! Ha ha ha haaaa ...'

Martina finishes with a tinkly laugh, obviously hoping it will be her out-line, but no, the floor manager is now indicating to her to fill for another few seconds.

And I'm thinking: Ring? I have a massive sparkler in my pocket ...

'Last word anyone?' Martina asks desperately, even though we have just been there.

'Yes,' I find myself saying, 'I just want to say hello to my fiancé; coincidental to what we've just been saying, we got engaged this morning.'

I flash my hand, nonchalantly exposing the M&S ring I've just jammed on my finger.

Kian and Martina gape at me, and we cut to a commercial break.

I win!!! Do I? Oops, what have I done?

The smell of burning fish distracts from the awkward moment.

'Will someone turn off that feckin' hot plate,' a voice shouts. Someone runs across the studio behind us. Then the floor manager is upon us, urgently waving Kian and I off the sofa so he can do the set-up for the next item.

'See ya,' Kian says gruffly to Martina as he heads off, impatiently pulling the mic from his shirt as he goes.

'Nice one,' she retorts.

Somehow he and I still manage to carry on the ignoring.

'And congratulations, Mary,' she turns to me, 'let's have a look at the ring.'

I sort of flick my hand across her gaze. The ring is such a gaudy heap, she'll think either I'm marrying a delusional cheapskate or it's real, and I've bagged a sheik or something similarly obscure. *Or* she'll know in an instant that I have just told a big saddo fib. She probably senses it already; she's the kind of woman who has sharp radar for that kind of thing. To cover my rising embarrassment I say, 'Strange discussion, went a bit off the topic and onto me, I felt.'

Normally I wouldn't bother expressing irritation over such an interview; the world hardly turns on a few pundits giving their tuppence worth. And saying it now in the middle of the show is bad form, I know.

'Oh really. I wouldn't have said that myself. Anyhow …' she's pissed off, but we can't go into it because our exchange is interrupted by Ronan sauntering over and collapsing on the couch beside her.

'Congratulations, when's the big day?' he asks warmly.

'Ah, it won't be for a while yet, you know what some fellas are like,' I answer. *Yeah, you know how hard it can be with some fellas, particularly the imaginary ones.*

He wishes me luck and happiness and I thank him. He turns to Martina to apologise for the odour of burnt fish that now fills the studio.

The wheelchair ladies are lined up into their starter positions for the next item. Chowder to disability – wow, the whole gamut of issues from c to d in a single afternoon.

Clodagh gives me an on-the-spot contract to sign for my hundred and twenty euro appearance fee. I remind her that I also need a taxi voucher for getting back into town. I've been leaping in and out of cabs today like I've the purse of a Paris Hilton. With a wink and a wave, Clodagh shoves three in my hand and then she's back to studio business. As I leave, they're back on air. Ronan's sleepy voice follows me to the door:

'It may be accident, illness or genetic, but whatever renders a woman wheelchair bound, without a doubt she will at some stage be left wondering one thing: How DO I stay fashionable when I'm in a permanent sitting down position? We asked our resident stylist, Bernie Doyle, to take three paraplegics around the shops to come up with three different contemporary looks that are as funky as they are comfortable. Wheel out there ...'

Ah, so that explains why the Massey Ferguson woman was wearing pedal pushers, a hoodie and a bandana. I leave Martina and Ronan in their la la la la loopy world and head out into reality.

CHAPTER 8

It's 3:10pm already. Next stop is the Westbury to interview Paddy
Finn, and I still have no information on him. It'll take what, fifteen
minutes at most in the taxi from here to Grafton Street? I switch
my mobile back on, order a taxi to be at reception in twenty minutes – should be there in half an hour. And instead of heading out
the security door and into the foyer, as I ought, I sneak back along
the corridor towards make-up. Hang a right, a left, run up the
back stairs, through the bowels of the newsroom into the belly of
light entertainment. I'm looking for any vague acquaintance with
the loan of a friendly computer. I need that comic's press release.

Nope, there's no one I know, or would ask at any rate. I scoot
along apace, don't want anyone asking me what I'm up to. Tech-
nically speaking, I'm trespassing, but feck it, who's going to shop
me?

The atmosphere is chilled, and I try to follow suit. I find myself
near my old desk, and, halleluiah, am I delighted to see that the
whole area is free. The production team are probably off at a
meeting, or enjoying, en masse, fresh afternoon scones and tea in
the canteen. Ah, the joys of semi-State: the endless carefree coffee
breaks, the chips-with-everything subsidised lunches, the never-

any-need-to-buy-your-own-stationery-ever-again luxury of it.

I know my way around the computers here, I know where to find the single office printer when I press 'p', I know what it feels like to feel at home here, but I absolutely don't belong here anymore. My hands are shaking as I bring up the google search page. I just want to get out of here as quickly as possible. Being here is bringing back all the badness of last year. Pathetic, but I literally feel tears in my eyes.

Steady, Mary, deep breaths. At least I'm going to get my stash of Paddy info. I'll speed read it in the taxi, look like I'm well up on him when we meet; there's probably nothing more insulting than someone turning up to interview you who can barely get your name right, let alone ask an intelligent question about your work. But here I am: I'm on top of things, a sensation I rarely feel, unless I'm with Rory, who has to be the laziest lover in the world.

I've just managed to type 'Paddy Fi' when I hear a flurry of footsteps behind me and then the voice hits like a mugger's wallop: 'No, no, no. You are completely and utterly wrong'. Ah, the unmistakable sentiment, the epic bitterness, the familiar tsunami of depression it engenders as it approaches. It's short, it's charmless, it confuses bullying with leadership and shouting with strength – welcome to the stage The Poison Dwarf, Attracta Butt. Ah, for Christ's sake, this is too stupid to credit.

I'm in a corner, there's no escape route, and I've no option. I dive under a desk and cower. When she's seated at hers, I'll slip quietly away.

But actually, it won't be that easy. Because, plot-sickeningly thickening, it's her bloody desk I've taken as my refuge. The stumpy legs are within an arm's length of me.

'Paddy Fi, who's Paddy Fi? And who's been googling at *my* desk?'

And a fee, a fi, a foe and a fum. Her voice really is extraordinary. It sounds like she's talking through her nose and it resents the imposition.

Now she has pressed 'search' and is vocal in her disgust at what comes up. Something about agriculture, apparently...

'Grain/seedling/1998/Genetech preys on the Paddy Fi,' she reads aloud:

'GRAIN is an international non-governmental organization which promotes the sustainable management and care of agricultural bio-diversity based on people's ...'

She clicks off the page when she's reached the end of the intro.

'Right. If there's a bleeding heart liberal amongst you, be warned: you can cry over cut flowers in your own time, but I am not having any of the Birkenstock brigade on my programme. So don't even ask. Not interested ! Not on my watch! End of story. I thought that was already abundantly clear.'

There's a silence; obviously no one knows what the hell she's on about, except me!

'Attracta?'

'What?'

One of her minions has a question. Please God she'll move in the direction of it. No, her shoes move toward me, she's taken her seat, she's tucked herself into her desk. That's the old Attracta technique at work: turn your back on whoever you're talking to, if they're lower in the pecking order. Keep 'em in their place. Think Genghis Khan in a twinset. Her shoes are in my face. Ordinary runner-type yokes, plain, flat, nondescript. They look like something you might pick up in Penneys, fifteen euro a pair for mucking about the house. But ah, ha, there's more. There's the little *Owen de Maguire Sport* label tucked, discreet but obvious, along the lip. 'These might look like nothing but that's not what they cost', is what they say: Well-to-wear Attracta, and how apt.

I bunch myself as tightly cornered under her desk as is possible. She's crossed her legs and the loose foot bobs up and down in tandem with the staccato of her conversation.

'Just call him back, say he's expected on the show, there was a verbal agreement. Don't take no for an answer...' Still terrorising her researchers.

An ugly runner narrowly misses my face on each beat of the above. What am I going to do? I could be here all afternoon at this rate. I check my watch: the taxi will be here in five minutes. Think, Mary, think ... then I don't need to think because my phone rings. I am having a heart attack, my life is flashing in front of me, prickles of intense embarrassment assault my scalp. I am about to be discovered, humiliated, and forever linked in everyone's mind with this abysmal incident.

My mobile has the shrill ring of an old fashioned telephone. Chosen not for the irony, ha ha, but for the volume, deaf, deaf. I've had a horror of missing a mobile call. Up until now. So this baby is loud. Loud enough to be heard over the roar of twin jet engines, the batter of a jack hammer, the hubbub of the office wherein you're trying to be deathly quiet and hide.

I scrabble for the phone in my bag, find it, see on the ID that it's Mam. She never calls on the mobile. Is something wrong? I get a flash of her gasping last breaths as she grabs for an out-of-reach inhaler. I turn the phone off. OK, it's my fault if Mammy dies, but right now, I'm the one who's dead. The phone rang long and so loud that it has has brought a hush to the office bustle.

'What the ... ' Attracta Butt is saying as her chair flies back and her head swings down, her interrogative eyes met by mine. There's a moment where we say nothing, just stare at each other. A moment for me to absorb how beyond idiotic I look, a moment for her to register her surprise, aversion, invasion; a moment for each of us to take in each other's reactions.

'Fuck?' is what she finally says.

'Ermm,' I say, thinking quick. In an effort to salvage my dignity, I attempt to get into the all-fours position and clamber free of her desk. I bang my head in the process, and find my path blocked by her loathed leg.

'You?' she asks, leaving me to figure the correct answer.

'Yes,' I say, going for the obvious one. My head is sore and I want to rub it, but I can't because I'm cramped up. Being made to feel small like this, but maybe not so literally, was an experience I grew used to when working for Ms Butt.

'Stand-up to her,' Rory was always saying, 'stand-up for your-self'. 'Just stand-up, even,' I'm thinking now. I'm imprisoned by her position, locked in a crouch. Everyone else in the office is looking over. I try to maintain some modicum of decorum by reversing back under the desk. I'm now staring out and up at eve-ryone. I am a dog. Still, 'hiya Frank,' I say to one of the heads I know.

He nods in reply, smiling tightly. Relieved, I suppose, that I didn't just say 'woof'.

'I know exactly what you're doing,' Attracta shrills. 'I am calling security right now. I will let them deal with you. They are permit-ted to search you. If you have any "Late Jape" information on your person it will be confiscated. But that's not all. No. Let me assure you I will be pursuing this matter through the official legal channels. This is a criminal offence and will be treated as such by "The Late Jape" production team,' she reams off. She has become Officious Automaton Poison Dwarf. She picks up her phone, bashes in an extension number, all the while blocking my exit.

I am having an out-of-body experience. Like my namesake Mary I am ascending slowly heavenward. But unlike The Virgin One, I only get as far as the ceiling tiles. I look down at myself. Cowering, uncomfortable, my enormous green handbag crumbled beside me, big hair ruined and potential substitute 'career' likewise.

I know what's going on. Attracta assumes I want to get back at her for what she did to me, because of what I did to her. The tit-for-tat curse of The Poison Dwarf! As if I could be arsed with any of it anymore? Revenge is a dish best served cold, they say, but in my experience by the time you've let it cool you've forgotten about it and it turns to a moldy heap, lost in the pantry of the past. That's where I'm at, but try and explain that to Butt-face as she waits for the person on the other end to pick up? Don't think so. She thinks I'm out to kill her baby: 'Pratt's Late Jape' – chat show; new; unprecedented ratings, attributed to the soft charisma of host Bryan Pratt, thirty going on seventy-five, blinding star in the RTÉ firmament.

Rumour has it that TV3 is planning to go head-to-head with a similar chat show, with hipper host, Dugsy O'Reagan, thirty going on eighteen, DJ and lead singer of the band The Fellas. I have insider information – Rory just happens to be their manager. I know the rumour is true. So does The Stumpy One, I'm sure. Bryan and Dugsy will soon be killing each other for the same pool of celebs, fighting over whoever's on the circuit promoting whatever shite they're promoting. Nobody wants to end up with the guy from Offaly talking about his hive design that has taken the bee-world by storm. Everyone wants Darren O'Marra, when he is home for a breather, talking about how helter-skelter strato-spherically well everything is going for him in the filums and the lurve/bonking department.

So, get it? Attracta thinks I'm on some sort of spying mission for Rory, as a revenge for what she did to me, or something along those lines. Talk about conspiracy theories, she'll be setting an albino monk on me in a minute.

It is clear that I am in deep dung. There's only one logical thing to do: I pray. St Jude – how did that novena go again?

In this the most vile of circumstances, I humbly beseech thee to intercede for me in thy capacity re: the hopeless case that is my pre-dicament and being clearly the plaintiff in this matter I wish to file divine proceedings pursuant to a celestial injunction to be served forthwith and let it out and let it in, hey Jude begin ...

Feck it, I just go for the general lapsed Catholic in a bind: Please God, please God, please God, please God, please God ...

As the man said, when the plane's crashing, no one's an atheist. Who are you going to appeal to, The Big Bang Theory? Please God, please God, please God, please God, please God ...

'Hello, we have a security situation. Could you send somebody up here immediately,' I hear Attracta say. Her voice sounds far away. All is lost. And then suddenly it's not!

'Well, what *is* the extension number for security then?' she snaps. Her voice is close again. I am back with myself, under the desk, I have an extra half a minute and therein lies an opportunity. And God is hearing me, he truly is! Because out of nowhere He appears in the flesh, in the office! GOD, aka Bryan Pratt, has just walked in, his shining €400000-a-year halo briefly blinding all present, his slightly buck-toothed smile and his lovely jumper and slacks and his lovely Louth charm bestowing themselves like a blessing on those gathered here together.

'Hello, how are ye?' he says unto the assembled, in his lovely accent.

A heavenly chorus of sopranos sings out from on high:

𝕳𝖆𝖑𝖑-𝖊-𝖑𝖚𝖎𝖆𝖍! 𝕳𝖆𝖑𝖑𝖊𝖑𝖚𝖎𝖆𝖍! 𝕳𝖆𝖑𝖑𝖊𝖑𝖚𝖎𝖆𝖍! 𝕳𝖆𝖑𝖑-𝖊𝖊𝖊-𝖑𝖚—𝖎𝖆𝖍!!!

But, in fairness, I'm probably the only one hearing that.

'How are ye all doin'?' he repeats.

Attracta lowers the phone and rises in an automatic trance to answer his call to conversation.

'Grand,' she says, colloquialising her language down to his popular-with-the-punters level. 'Can I get you a wee cup of tea?' she offertorys, more or less genuflecting.

This is the flip side of the producer who treats their team like dog pooh: the deep need to compensate by licking the star arse at every opportunity. The ratings all hang on this one man. Attracta-Career-Minded would roll out her own tongue for him in lieu of a red carpet if the situation ever arose. While she's distracted with idolatry, I take my chances.

I'm out from under the desk and off across that office like a kinetic rabbit out of the hatches at Shelbourne Park. There's no stopping me now.

Like the hound dog she is, Attracta sniffs my escape, but she's too late. I'm chasing down the stairwell as she shouts to no one in particular, 'stop that … that … thing!' There's an expletive playing on her lips, but in front of His Holiness Bryan she censors herself.

'Oh, Holy God!' I hear him exclaim behind her.

What would I say to security anyway – look, check, there's nothing in my bag. By the time they'd have gone through everything, Paddy Finn would have turned to dust in the Westbury. No – I am going to be on time, against all odds.

CHAPTER 9

The theme tune from *Chariots of Fire* accompanies me in my head as I dash out the back of the office, across the set and props hangar. I sprint past the shiny high-tech wheel of 'Your Chance Mrs', through the resting sofas of 'Pratt's Late Jape', past the backdrop of RTÉ's own original take on a popular cookery programme: 'Ready, Steady, Bake', through the styrofoam Grecian pillars of the politics programme, 'The Important Show' ... Lucky I know my way around. Scouting all the while for the boys in brown, I dash past the back of the canteen, across the lawns, past the radio centre and slow as I come along by the exteriors set of 'Dirty Ol' Town', the flagship soap. There's a scene being shot, actors and crew standing around in the drizzle, ploughing through the script in the usual series of one-take wonders. Must look normal, must look normal. I glance over at 'the action', like you would.

'Welcome to the land of make-believe,' one of the characters who plays one of the characters said to me the first time I came down this way to gawk at the famous sham street.

Make-believe? Make believe to my mind is yellow brick roads and feather boas, not the 'Jimmy's on the smack, I was a battered wife for years, but now I'm having an affair with an illegal alien, he's black as the ace of spades, I'm pregnant, he's being deported and me husband just found the whole thing out. Will you have a cup of tea?' of 'Dirty Ol' Town'. A huge swathe of the population is glued to it, life elevated to less than it is. And it's all shot in wondrous cheap Tellyscope: the shuddering walls, the background copse of wooden extras, the quick-fix lighting that gives everyone indoors a three-way shadow that follows them around like a paranormal alter-ego.

I see my friend of the 'make-believe' comment across from me in his greasy vest, shaking a spanner at the camera, acting for Ireland. I'm so busy trying to be normal that I trip in a pothole and twist my ankle. 'Ow!' All heads shoot in my direction. 'Stop!' the director shouts. (No fancy declarations of 'cut' here; the language is as humdrum as the drama.) I limp on, embarrassed by my faux pas, anxious not to be recognized. I know the director, too – don't ask. The security man on the edge of the action glances at me sharply. Was that his walkie-talkie I heard buzzing? It's all I can do not to break into a run.

The back gate to RTÉ is just up the path and round the corner. It comes into view, escape framed by bunches of leafy laurel bushes. Except it's not escape, because it's locked. The world has become a terrifying place since 9/11 and you need a security swipe to get in and out here now. I'll just have to wait 'til someone legit appears with a pass. I check my watch. It's a quarter to four. Feck. The taxi was due at reception five minutes ago. I'm taking out my mobile to track down my transport when I hear a footfall in the gravel behind.

Intuitively I dive into the bushes. Could be security and I can't take chances. I crouch in the laurels, the accumulated drizzle on the waxy leaves treating me like an honorary sponge, my modest heels sinking in undergrowth and compost, twigs of other, higher up shrubs snagging the lacquered masterpiece of my hair, and what can only be a crust of dried bird pooh attaching itself to my lapel.

'Hello,' says my phone. It's the taxi company answering my call. In a whisper that's barely audible even to me, I explain my taxi predicament. But thanks to the famed efficiency of everything to do with transport in Dublin, my cab is still 'on its way'. I redirect it to pick me up outside Donnybrook church. 'Donnybrook church. Donnybrook church.' I have to spit-whisper into the phone several times before the taxi operator has got it and repeated it back to me. 'Ohhh, Donnybrook Church.'

'Yes, Donnybrook Church, Donnybrook Church,' I'm re-repeating when another voice interjects.

'Is there somebody in there?' It's male, posh-Irish, boomingly confident. Not security then, T.G. But what to do? What to do? Quick-thinking, I scoop up some soggy earth and crumble it lightly over my phone.

'Yes, yes,' I laugh loudly and nonchalantly, bending and reversing out of the scrub. If the first thing he claps his eyes on is my very womanly arse, he might be distracted from the male suspicion his tone implied. I do a few little helpless feminine ohhs and ahhs as I extricate myself and bag from the foliage. 'Yes, I lost this in the bushes, silly me!' I declare, as I turn to face him, presenting my phone as evidence. 'Ohh, it got all dirty,' I say in breathy distress, as I limply shake it to loosen off the dirt I just planted.

'Oh, ermm, I, see, yes,' he says, a bit embarrassed, a bit confused. He's an older man, well dressed, formal, dignified. The arse-plan worked. It's as if he has just indiscreetly burst in on me at my private ablutions.

'I was just heading out,' I add quickly, provoking a move-on before he has time to deconstruct the logic of suddenly losing your phone in the middle of a hedge.

'Right, right, me too. Allow me,' he says, as he produces and swipes his tag across the security check. The gate clicks and he opens and holds it for me as I pass through.

'Thank you very much,' I say.

'So–' he begins saying when we're both safely on the outside.

'Sorry,' I cut across him, 'in a terrible hurry.' And I run away from him, limping on my tender ankle. *Hurry, hurry.* I know I look stupid – Taxi, Westbury, Paddy Finn, job, professional, me – this is all that's on my mind as I leg it round to the front of Donny-brook church, where, thank you, God, my taxi awaits.

'Hope you weren't waiting long,' I pant breathlessly to the driver.

'Nah, just got here. Where to?'

'Westbury Hotel. Top of Grafton Street will do. And umm, I wonder could you hurry, I've to be there by four.'

'Well, I'll see what I can do, Mrs. But this is not the Tardis. It's four minutes to four already.'

Is it? Feck. I hate being late, although you wouldn't know that as such from my timekeeping record. I take out my notebook to string a few questions together for Mr Finn. Now, how to get him to spill the comedy beans for twenty minutes without the fact that I know next to nothing about him raising its ugly head? Q. One, what's the show about? Good. Q. Two ... My phone rings. It's Mam. I answer at once, glad that she's not dead, and guilty that I'd forgotten the potential crisis.

'Mam, hi. Are you all right? Sorry I couldn't answer before, I–'

'Am I all right? No. No, I am not all right is the answer to that question, if you must know.'

'What's up, is it your asthma again?' She certainly sounds fine, if a bit miffed for some reason.

'What's up? Do you need even to ask that question? How do you think I feel when my only daughter announces on national television that she has got engaged, and I'm sitting there like a fool, the last to know.'

Oh. Oh. The lie I let fly on 'Afternoon Stew' is coming home to roost. I'm tempted to just hang up and deal with this later. But I don't. I can't.

'I thought you had a committee meeting or something. You weren't even going to watch me on telly?'

'We were in Maureen Doohan's house, I said you were on, so of course she turned on the TV. And there I was with the six other ladies on The Committee, including Deirdre Gannon who is a right old 'b' and only too delighted to see the look on my face as you, sitting there with your hair like a lunatic, hold up your hand and show the ring to Ireland without having the decency to come down here to Claredunny and tell Mammy first. Well, thank you very much. Is that all the thanks I get? And who is he anyway? Let me guess. That Rory who has been using you and stopping you from meeting a nice man you could settle down with. I never liked him and now he's family.'

'Mam, Mam, listen. I can't talk now. It's a long story, but trust me, I am *not* engaged.'

There's silence at the other end of the line as she takes in this information.

'So it's all off then already?' she says finally, sounding almost disappointed.

'It's not "all off already"; it was never on. Look, I'll explain later, OK?'

Then I have to cut her off.

'Sorry, Mam, I'm working. I have to go. I'll call you later, OK? It's nothing. Love you.'

I wait a millisecond for reciprocation, and when it's not forthcoming I hang up.

'Broken engagement?' the taxi driver interjects. 'Happened to meself, awful bloody mess. I was … '

A heartbreak confessional is the last thing I need.

'Yeah, sorry, can't talk about it right now,' I say.

'Ah, I understand, love,' he says. 'Don't worry, you'll get over it.' He flashes me a consoling look in the rear view mirror.

Rory – Mam automatically assumed it was Rory I had gotten engaged to. Hilarious. Isn't it? Why? When I first saw Rory I thought I didn't have a chance in hell. I had his number, but did I use it? Did I go for it? No! And then fate, or just Dublin. I met him again, I remember, at a casual crowded house party in Rathmines. There was I, can of Carlsberg in hand, propped against the wall of coats in the hall, and there, suddenly, was Rory, sauntering down the stairs. 'Wow. Again,' I thought when I looked up and saw that hair and those eyes and that body and its cool leather jacket coming at me. And this time, rather that run from the knee-melt, I pursued it. Call it Danish courage. I gulped back the can of beer I had in my hand, cracked open another in the kitchen, had a good slug of that and of a stray bottle of whiskey and a toke of a floating spliff, and then I went on the hunt for him.

I somehow managed to manoeuvre him into a one-on-one and managed to be ulta-chatty despite wanting to vomit with the excited stress of it all. Not only chat, but do all those flirty things magazines always tell you to do: occasionally touch your breasts as you speak, mirror his body language, pout when you're not speaking, agree with everything he says, let him do most of the talking, laugh your tits off when he says anything half funny. 'No way, the photocopier didn't break down, did it? Oh, ha, ha, ha, ha, ha, ha, ha, ha, ha, ha, ha.' Given the whole bag of tricks, he probably thought I had Parkinson's or something, but it worked.

We somehow found tons to talk about – Pigs – the band he was in with that day, and other bands and his job in general, and mine, and us and what we were all about. Soon it was clear that what we were all about was a preamble to first base. 'That's a nice necklace,' I remember him saying, as he fingered the beads around my neck. I thought I was going to spontaneously combust as his knuckles brushed my neck. There was definitely no such word as 'no' floating anyway near me when Rory suggested he accompany me to my bed. The taxi of love took us home and the rest is history.

Yes, I slept with him on the first night.

'Which is exactly what you should never ever ever ever ever do,' Dr Suzy Wurlerwitz says in her stupid book. Maybe she's right. 'At least six dates, twelve preferably, and get a reassurance you are his *exclusive* sexual partner – *first*'. But how can you apply these American rules in Ireland? Men and women don't *date* here, we go out for pints.

Exclusive pints, Rory?

The taxi stops. We're at the top of Grafton Street. 'Time heals everything,' the driver confides in me as I climb out. 'Thanks, I'll remember that the next time I have a hangover,' I tell him as I hand him a voucher and sign off for it. Then I turn to attack the street at a sprint. I slalom through the clog of shoppers, hang a left toward The Westbury, dodge the blooming buckets of the flower sellers and a gaggle of American tourists gathered around the statue of Phil Lynott. 'They got it wrong,' I overhear one remark, 'Lionel Richie is heavier than that.'

Ten minutes late, I'm racing up The Westbury's marble stairs. I land in the kitsch comfort of the first floor lounge. Tonnes of chandelier challenge the ceiling. An ancient man sporting a velvet dickie tickles the baby grand. 'There's no business like show business' is the ghost of the melody you can just about catch in his verveless recital. It delicately ripples into the tinkle of china and civilised whisper of conversation, before sinking into the swirly abyss of the carpet. There's an air of up-market mental hospital about the place. And in amongst the neat ladies supping on afternoon tea and nice fancies, sits my man, Paddy. He's wearing glaringy expensive runners teamed with casually swanky jeans and a grey sweatshirt under a blue t-shirt – a look that says 'I'm just another bloke, not really'. His head is hidden by a tabloid, a red top.

'Sorry,' I address him through the newsprint. 'I think perhaps you've been waiting for me.'

No response.

I tap the paper.

It descends slowly, a curtain opening down to reveal Mr Paddy Finn, star. Hair is the first impression, great bunches of it battling on his head – is it going this way or that, are those waves or full curls, is it dirty or is that just the colour? And underneath these hairy conundrums, another: the face itself. It carries the voltage of being semi-famous, but its bland laddishness begs the question, why? How? Everything about it says 'very ordinary' – the narrow lips of the average mouth, the nondescript button of a nose and the eyes – two gobs of grey-blue suspended in orbs of a red-white watery swill – tired but sharp at the same time. He has a day-old stubble and a mish-mash air that suggests late-nights, booze, sex, drugs, world weariness, superiority, coupled with possible future death by smoking-induced cancer. 'Oh, he thinks he's great,' they'd say about him down in Claredunny: the killer comment.

Is he a cliché – say, young enough when he hit the big time to think he knew everything because he was palmed a free gram now and again, and long enough doing well to think he has done everything because he once slept with eleven different women on two different continents in one week and he couldn't recall the names of any of them when he got home to his fiancée?

I've got to get some copy to save my arse.

I say, 'hello, you must be Paddy Finn, and I'm late. Sorry.'

'Oh right, yeah,' he drawls.

He has the delivery of a ninety-year-old man. Does he have some sort of debilitating disease? Premature loss of the ability to hold a conversation?

'Sorry,' I say again. It's twenty past four already. I introduce myself.

'Fine, yeah, OK, good. But can we be, like, quick. I hate doing interviews,' he mutters, pushing his hand through the conglomeration of his hair.

'Sure thing. Can I get you anything?' I offer.

'Yeah. I'd love some tea and a bun.'

Am I on expenses? I forgot to ask Miriam.

'Will a scone do?' I ask.

'I'd like something spongy with cream, and icing, actually,' he says.

Ah, so not as casual as he looks; a man who knows what he wants, and wants to get it. Cream buns it is so.

I'm standing over him as we have this conversation, feeling like a waiter. He's quite comfortable with that dynamic, I notice. I wave to an actual waiter and order buns and tea for two. I do a recce for a seat. The only free sit-able on thing is a footstool. I pull it over and position myself by Paddy. With him semi-reclined in his one-and-a-half seater, it looks like I'm here to deliver some sort of therapy: listen to his troubles, do a manicure or merely lift a nearby cushion and fan him gently as he rests.

'What's news in England?' I ask, nodding to his paper as I pull my interview equipment out.

'Jordan has a big chest,' he says.

'Right.'

'Nice Walkman.'

'Ta.' It's an old yoke I borrowed off Declan when I went to have my chart read recently.

'Lo-tech,' Paddy comments.

'That's the kind of gal I am,' I tell him, in an attempt to break the ice. I give him what I think is a cute, 'I'm nice, you could like me' smile. He returns it with a blank stare that I take to mean 'yawn'.

'So, why do you hate doing interviews?' I begin.

He groans and slithers deeper into his chair. There's a pause, we look at each other, I'm waiting for more. Finally he says,

'Because I do.'

'Fair enough,' I say. 'So, tell me, what's your up-coming show about?'

As I ask this I touch my hand to my hair and find a stray twig from earlier. I'm tugging it out with difficulty as Paddy asks:

'What's it about?'

'Yeah,' I repeat, distracted.

'What do you mean, what's it about?'

'Erm, what is it, you know, aiming for, in the content. What are *you* aiming for?'

'I'm aiming to be funny,' he grumps.

'Good,' I say. 'Funny' I write on my crumpled pad. Thankfully, our petite buns arrive on their multi-story dish, with our pot of steaming tea, and setting the whole lot up involves much manoeuvring of dainty tables and delicate china. Soon Paddy is munching an iced fancy and gulping tea and looking happier. In a cake-for-answers trade off, he spontaneously tells me, 'I haven't played back here in Ireland for over a year, so that should be interesting.'

'For you or the audience?' I ask.

He gives me a silent stare-down before answering, 'Both, I hope'.

'Is that important to you?'

'What?'

'Being back here.'

'Of course. This is where I'm from.'

Well, hold the front page, Miriam – 'Comic considers his Irish roots important and could talk about anything in up-coming show' scoop. I can't help but get the feeling that I'm off to a horrible start. I cover my doubt by taking a long, considered slug of my tea. Right. Round two. Things can only get better.

'What's your show called again?' I ask, flicking through pages of my notebook as if the name is adrift in my sea of prepared

Paddy notes. I'm scanning old memos to 'remember tweezers' and 'Rory – chicken & potatoes, wine', while racking my brains for it. I know there's a title, I've seen it on his huge posters around town.

'Older,' he answers.

'Ah yes, that's it. Older. Of course. How old *are* you?'

'Twenty-nine.'

'Twenty-nine?'

'Yeah, next week.'

'Happy birthday.'

'Thanks.'

We talk about his schedule. He tells me that apart from the touring, he's had offers to write a novel, a screenplay, a sitcom, an opinion column, an advice column, just a *column*, a comic strip, an autobiography and manuals on how to be a modern man, a successful stand-up and sexy. 'But I'm just too busy, so I've said no to all of them except the first three.'

And he's just finished filming alongside Darren O'Marra in *Bottom Gear.* 'a hard-hitting, real to life, Dublin gangland film set in Cabra.'

'And what do you play?' I ask him.

'The ice-cream man.'

'Is that one of the gangsters?'

'No, he's the ice-cream man.'

'Right. What's Darren O'Marra like to work with?' I ask.

'Great bloke. Chilled. Cool. Good. Nice.'

He terminates the list of vague positives when I say, 'Grand'.

I ask him does he have a comedy hero. Yes, Zack Whammy, a hard-hitting, American stand-up, apparently. Angry, sharp, groundbreaking, dead.

'Why is he your hero?' I ask.

'Because he went places others feared to tread ... '

'The grave,' I laugh.

'Seriously, he had balls – the racist paedophile stuff – genius.'

'Absolutely,' I agree, just to be on the safe side. I think I've heard of Zack Whammy before; something about him throwing stuff out of a hotel window, a telly, or a cat or his girlfriend or something. I'm not sure enough to bring it up. I ask him does he model his approach to comedy on Zack or any other comic.

'No,' he says, ' you cannot do that and be authentic.'

'Authenticity, that's important to you,' I say.

'Yeah,' he says, affirming the fuzzy statement.

'But don't you think you're a bit young to be talking about being older?' I find myself asking him.

'What, you mean calling my show "Older"?'

'Yeah.'

'Well I've been doing stand-up for nearly ten years.'

'So you're old in comedy years?' I ask.

'Yeah, I suppose.'

'How do they co-relate to ordinary human years?'

'Erm,' he considers the facetious question. 'I'd say one human year equals 2.5 comic years: one to two and a half.'

'So that makes you what? Seventy-two and a half?'

'Yeah, you're quick at sums – that's what it feels like, anyway.'

'Right. And that means someone like Joan Rivers must be pushing, what? Two hundred years of age?' I ask, trying to keep it going.

'That'd be about right,' he agrees.

'Hence the legendary status ... '

' ... and the facial reconstruction ... '

' ... but who can blame her. Wouldn't you, too, if you were a hundred and seventy-five?'

This is good, I'm thinking, we're on a roll, finally. Then my phone rings. I answer it automatically. It's Monica.

'Hi, saw you on television this afternoon,' she says. There's an edge to her voice. Something's coming – what is it now? Well, whatever it is, she might have time to chat. But I don't.

'You saw it, that's great,' I say, quickly. Hoping she'll pick up the urgency in my voice.

'Yeah, we have a television in the studio, so we all watched,' she says. And? Where is this conversation going? Is she waiting for me to say something?

'Great, that's really great. Thanks for watching. Look. I've got to go now. I'm actually in the middle of something, so I'll–'

'Your engagement thing–'

'My engagement ... oh, Jesus, I'll explain when–' She bulldozes across my laughter.

'I just can't believe you didn't tell me before just announcing it on television, I was talking to you this morning and everything; it left me feeling really odd. *Really* odd. We *really* have to talk. Are you suggesting it is who I think it is? I just cannot believe–'

'OK, look, I've said I'm busy and I am, so no disrespect but I am going to have to terminate this call right now,' I say sharply, noticing Paddy drift back to his newpaper.

My tone silences Monica.

'OK?' I check before I ring off.

'OK.'

'See you at 6:20 then.'

'6:35,' she says, and she's gone.

'So, how did you get into comedy?' I zip straight in, trying to get us back to where we were in the interview.

My answer is another groan.

'Don't ask me that. Can't you think of a more original question?'

'Can't you think of a more original answer?' I persist.

'OK, all the other buses were full, so I got on the one that said comedy,' he says.

'How do you feel about being considered a sex symbol?' I ask him. I'm just guessing that he is, and he mentioned the offer to write a *How to be Sexy* manual. He certainly wouldn't be my cup of tea. You can imagine that he was the class mouth at school, he's still got that youthful smart-aleck air about him. But when you've left the school gates behind, that kind of demeanour doesn't seem cool anymore to me; it seems sort of ... regressive. But Rory has told me you could take a three-headed, pustulous hunchback leper, put him behind a mic on a stage, and if he's anyway funny the groupies will be gathering on their knees at the door. That theory, he says, is based on observation.

'Great. My wife loves the idea,' he says.

'You're married?' I ask.

'Yeah, three months ago, we're expecting our first in the summer.'

'Baby?'

'Yeah.'

I'm surprised. He doesn't look the dad type. He looks too young – that whole 'young pup' thing.

'You have kids yourself?' he asks me.

Ah, the inevitable question. You hit your mid-thirties and suddenly it seems every second day there's an occasion worthy of the question, with its implicit *and why not?* I'm always surprised that people think I look like the kind of woman who *could* have a clatter of kids at home. I associate that with being *older*, but I suppose I *am* the one that's older now. I give my well honed standard answer:

'No.'

He seems a bit disappointed, as if I've robbed him of a 'what's it like' information opportunity.

'I'm not married either,' I tell him.

'Yeah, I gathered from your telephone conversation,' he says.

'Oh, that,' I laugh, 'that is so stupid, I was on this television pro-gramme this afternoon and ... ah, never mind.'

'What? Tell me,' he asks.

'Believe me, you don't want to know,' I say, surprised by his interest.

'No, I do,' he says.

'OK,' I say, and I end up telling him about my fiasco on 'After-noon Stew', which of course leads into being caught under Attrac-ta's desk, which goes on to the story of The Poison Dwarf and 'Attitude' and how and why I ended up interviewing him here today ... 'and so, to be brutally honest, I don't actually know that much about you', I finish, bringing it back to being here with him now.

'That's some story,' he says, 'and you know what, there's not that much to know about me. All you need are the dates of my show in Curate's Lane. Put that in the paper and I'm happy. Cool.'

'OK.'

I'm presuming that's the end of the interview. I'm mildly embarrassed that we've culminated on my confessional, that it seems to have ground us to a halt. But, surprisingly, the opposite happens.

'You know,' he continues, 'I'll tell you something – I hate doing interviews because I hate having to sell myself to sell my shows. I hate having to package up a version of myself and hand it to people like you. I hate the way you guys spin your own hang-ups and shit into that package when you write it up. I don't want to add my mug to the barrage of public faces. I don't want people who I don't know thinking they know me. I don't want to add another fake persona to the public bullshit of what it means to be a human being and alive now, because it *is* all bullshit, it's all sell, sell, sell. I'm not in this to sell myself, I'm in this because it's my work, it's my vocation. That's what I meant about being *authentic*. That's what I'm trying to do. Trade in the truth. That's what I'm about, I'm a Truth Trader. There you go.'

As suddenly as he began his outburst, he stops. His words seem to echo on.

'I'm not for sale,' he adds quietly, an afterthought.

We each sip the last of our tea.

'And I have a sense of *enoughness*, you know what I mean?'

'No,' I say.

'I mean I have a threshold when I know I have *enough*. I don't want to be greedy, you know? Enough is enough for me, see what I'm saying?'

This time I say 'yes'.

'So have you reached the "enough" point' yet?' I ask.

'No.'

'OK.'

We silently sip tea again.

I say 'good' in an effort to wrap things up nicely.

'Good?' he repeats.

'Yeah, that's really interesting stuff,' I say.

'Have I given you enough rope to hang me?' he asks.

'Maybe you've been stitched up in the past, but that's not my style,' I tell him.

'How do you know, you said you're new at this game?' he insists.

'Because it's not,' I argue succinctly, 'why are you so defensive?'

'Experience,' he tells me.

Again, I assume we're about to conclude, but he elaborates with a story of an interview he did around the time of the Asian tsunami. He and the interviewer got sidelined discussing how much aid corrupt bureaucrats in the affected countries would siphon off, and what could you give that wouldn't be nicked. When the interviewer then asked Paddy if he were donating anything himself he'd jokingly said yeah, he had arranged to send a container of chocolate swiss rolls to Indonesia. They'd laughed about it together. Next day the headline: "LET THEM EAT CAKE": Irish Comic on Tsunami Victims' appeared. He ended up having to issue a round of humiliating apologies.

'Shit,' I agree with him.

'Yeah, and that was the end of me in Banda Aceh Province,' he drolls, making me laugh, 'anyway, I'm out of here, man, I've to be somewhere else five minutes ago.'

'Anything else you want mentioned?' I ask him,

'A DVD is being recorded during this run and it will be in the shops later in the year. Maybe you could stick that in?'

'OK.'

'Cheers, Maggie,' he says as he creaks to a stand and brushes the crumbs from his clothes. 'I guess I'm just going to have to trust you,' he says finally, before he slouches off into the grey afternoon.

Love many, trust few, my father voice tells me.

'Nice meeting you,' I call after him.

I snap off the recorder. I quite enjoyed all that, I think to myself. Pleased, I exit the hotel with a skip in my step. The bun and the chat seem to have cured my aching ankle.

'Excuse me, excuse me,' a voice pants behind me and a finger taps me on the shoulder. It's the waiter from upstairs.

'Your bill?'

CHAPTER 10

I'm back out in the whirl of Grafton Street again when the phone rings. It's Declan.

'I see skies of blue,' he sings.

'Hello, hello, how did it go?' I ask him through the song, but he doesn't pause to answer me.

'... and I think to myself, what a wonderful world.'

Which he repeats fortissimo and largo and irritating-o:

'And I think to myself, WHAT A WONDERFUL WORLD.'

'You got it, I take it. Well done, congratulations.'

'Better than that.'

'There's more?' I ask, confused.

'There's less, AND THAT'S MORE, as they say.'

'Sorry, Declan, what are you saying?'

'I walked.'

'You *walked?*'

'These boots were made for walking ...' he sings.

I'm not in the mood for this.

'Just tell me what you're telling me straight or I'm going to hang up,' I say sharply.

'I walked out on the pitch. On my job. On the whole Hades.'

'What?'

'I walked out and burnt those bridges and I FEEL GOOD,' he's singing again.

'Where are you now?'

'I'm just sitting here with Kavanagh by the-leafy-with-love banks of the canal; we're growing with nature again as before we grew.'

He's near Baggot Street bridge, at the Patrick Kavanagh statue, reciting school poetry. It could be worse, he could actually be in the canal. I wouldn't put it past him. Not to drown, you understand, just to go for a celebratory swim.

'Do you want to meet up?' I ask.

'Yeah,' he says immediately, 'I'd like that.'

'Ohhkaay,' I think it through quickly. I've no option but to ask him to join Monica and me for dinner, and then maybe get him to come to the play? I can't meet him earlier, and if I leave it any later he'll just go and get plastered. So I invite him along. I ask him to join us at 6:50; Monica and I will have fifteen minutes for chat and patching up beforehand. She mightn't be too happy, but feck it. You gotta do the right thing. I can't legislate for her mood.

Declan's certainly on for dinner and a play.

'FAB-A-DOO-BIE!' he says.

Before I ring off I warn him to be sane.

In the interests of his mental health I make a detour to Dawson Street before heading home. I'm going to get some help for Declan, something of the *Lose Everything, Have It All,* or *Be Yourself, Not An Eejit* variety. Anything. There's a heap of it in the 'Spiritual/Healing' shelves of Waterstones. Browsing, I quickly conclude that Declan's issues are not answered by the *7 Steps To The Power of The Giant Within Who Feels The Fear but Dances With Friends and Influences*

People Anyway kind of thing. Any of that would just be further fuel to the fire of his scepticism, more blur to his lack of focus. I'm looking for something ... something like ... this, aha. Here we are now – I'm holding in my hand a pint-sized hard-backed cube of a book, entitled *The Book of Nuggets*. The blurb on the back contains the following instructions:

Holding the book firmly between two hands, concentrate on what it is that is troubling you. Hold that thought in your mind as you press the book over your heart and rotate it in a counter-clockwise direction. Now, stop. Take a deep breath. Open the book. Read the words. That is **your** *nugget.*

"Simple, profound, an *I Ching* for modern folk with no time." *The Cincinnati Review of Books.*

"*The Book of Nuggets* changed my life."

Anon.

This will do. I decide to road test it first, though. I get a raised furry eyebrow from a haggard academic-type in 'Political & Social Science'. Agreed, on the surface I may look like a woman humming to herself while stroking her chest with a small, fat hardback. But what's really going on is that I am asking The Great Energy Force That Unites Us All if Miriam will be happy with my Paddy Finn/Attitude column. Or not. Focus, focus, ignore that staring toddler. Now, open sesame! And my 'nugget' is:

Future is the way forward, usually.

Ah, feck it, I've no time to look for anything else. I dash over to the cash desk to pay for it. As I'm waiting for my laser slip, I notice The Jumper of Academe sidling over to where I was, trying to figure, no doubt, which book provoked the chest rub. One for a seminar with his freshers perhaps? I sign off another €17.99 and hurry home.

Time to get organised for tonight. On the hop, I ask the book what I should wear.

Slowly, at this time, it tells me. For some reason I start to run.

Panting, home, late as ever, I shower, exfoliate, foam, tone, scrub, moisturise, smooth, firm, intensify, refine, take years off, deodorise and fumigate with the full range of *Celtic Earth* that I got free last night and can't resist, even if I'll end up smelling like a creel of turf. Then I slaughter my eyebrows with plucker, slap on foundation, do eyes, do lips, mulch hair with fingers. Then, decision, decision: *Slowly, at this time.* What will I wear? OK, remember, you want to see Rory tonight. Make an effort – the new basque. I lace myself into it. *Sausage meat* I can't help thinking. Laced sausage. Exhaling and not breathing again, that seems to work. But will have to breathe again at some stage. Inconvenient, but a fact – like much of life. Jesus, was getting into this thing as difficult in the shop? Am I The Incredible Expanding Woman? But tied on, it's sexy, it's hot, even if it feels like something designed for the delectation of an Opus Dei penitent. I overlay it with a lacy wrap-around that cleverly camouflages my drumlins, and pull on my vintage tulle skirt – a skirt that says *frivolous!, girlie! curtains!* (in the wrong light). But add the killer heels, (that I rarely wear because they're a killer), and I've got the look: Thirtysomething glam in an understated, slightly overweight and unironed kind of way. A girl who's a bit of craic, a girl who's as likely to say, 'ah feck it, yeah, I'll have a seventh pint of Guinness' as 'gin and slimline, please'; a girl who's not afraid to say exactly what she wants (after three and half years silence on the matter). 'Tonight is the first night on the town of the rest of your life,' I tell myself as I practise in the shoes in front of the mirror.

'Rory, hi.' *Pause, let him take me in.* 'We've got to talk. Now.'

Or

'Rory, hi.' *Pause.* 'I think I love you.'

Or

'Rory, hi.' *Pause.* 'What? Yeah, I'd love a pint of Guinness.'

What *will* happen between me and Rory tonight? Hey, ask the book! I press it to my squashed breast. I pray for the right answer. I open it. I read, *Sit quietly and treat yourself to an over-hot muffin.*

Well, that's positive if it's anything. Happy, I shove the book in my bag to give to Declan and I hobble off into town in my torturous shoes.

CHAPTER 11

I arrive in Chumps on time. Derek directs me to the table. A pale woman with dark curly hair, green eyes, glossed thin lips and an attractive yet don't-fuck-with-me air about her is already there before me – that's Monica. She's not wearing her glasses; she looks  much more attractive without them. She looks like a pre-Raphaelite business woman – Millais's *Ophelia* after a hard day at the office. She's in shades of green wool and velvet, an outfit that looks like it came from Avoca Handweavers, but, knowing Monica, it's a one-off by some obscure but soon to successful designer. I feel edgy and unprepared somehow, as I move in for the 'hello'. 'Hi Monica, sorry I'm late,' I say.

Actually, I'm not late, she was early, but there you go.

'Hi,' she says, folding away the magazine she'd been reading.

'I like your outfit,' I say as I sit.

'I like your ... underwear thing,' she tells me.

We nod at each other.

'So.'

'So.'

'Look, I'm sorry ... ' she begins, as I begin,

'I'm sorry that ... '

Our two sorrys crash and stop.

'I'm sorry I got irritated with you last night. I don't even remember what it was over, to be honest. And I'm sorry I was snappy on the phone earlier, but I really was in the middle of something important.' I take the upper hand in the apologies, apologies, apologies department, 'But let me explain.' I recount my ridiculous 'Afternoon Stew' again, and suddenly tired of saying 'sorry', add that I was annoyed that she immediately jumped to the conclusion that I would compromise our friendship in *any* way, and furthermore that I was annoyed by our conversation earlier in the day – that we *had* said 6:20 originally. 'Look, I had it written down,' I say, even pulling my tattered diary from my handbag to point out this evidence. Having started, I decide I am going to finish.

'But that's only the tip of the iceberg,' I say. 'It felt to me that you were *ordering* me to visit Breege this morning. And it wasn't as life or death as you said. You put needless pressure on me. I was busy. My job is just as important as yours. It's not the first time you have done that, but the time has come for it to be the last. OK? You cannot treat me like that. That's not what I call a friendship.' I stop, exhausted but elated. Wow! I can't believe I just said all that. 'We need to talk this out, and we need to talk this out now,' I conclude. Then I remember, 'And we need to talk it out quickly, because Declan Twomey is joining us for dinner.'

Monica looks at me blankly. The silence following my outburst scares me. Then, in a very measured voice, Monica says, 'about what I was saying on the phone, I'll be honest, I thought it was Rory you were referring to on telly this afternoon. And I thought you ought to know, he's been cheating on you.'

'I know that,' I laugh, cutting across her, slightly annoyed at her upperhand tone and slightly humiliated at having to laugh this off again. It's not as if I haven't told her before, but I tell her again, 'we're not in an exclusive relationship; cheating doesn't come into it.'

'With me,' she says.

The words sink into me like a fist. The air is sucked from the room. There's a ringing in my ears. I'm stunned. There are tears threatening my eyes; tears of anger, disappointment, betrayal. All the familiar parameters of my life shift slightly under the force of this new information. I look at Monica. She's the same but different. I want to run, but I stay. I want to know everything and I want to know nothing. I just stare at Monica. She meets my gaze head on: nothing. She's daring me to react. I can't. I'm out of depth in my own life.

'What?' I say eventually.

'I'm seeing Rory,' she says, 'and it's serious.'

'Serious?' I repeat. As if my three-and-a-half-year involvement with him wasn't? As if, fundamentally, I'm not and she is? This theme is a repeat of so many things in our fifteen-year friendship. She's the one saying, 'yeah, I know that already' when I reach what I think is an amazing deduction on how things really work; she's the one saying in so many words 'I told you so' when I fuck up. Let's face it, she's the one we probably both take more seriously than me. I want to go. All I can think of to do right now is RUN AWAY. My body is about to follow my made-up mind when Declan arrives. He fluthers in on a high.

Monica could squeeze in a quick 'sorry' before his effusion bombards us, but she chooses not to. She's not sorry, I realise in a flash. She's into Rory and not about to get out. She's won. Again.

'HELLO, HELLO, HELLO, two women alone. Allow me to introduce myself. I am your friend come to break bread and share an evening at the knee of Thespis. Mary, kiss, kiss, and Monica HELLO, you look FABADOOBIE.'

He doesn't read the atmosphere, of course. He reaches over and pecks each of us on the cheek as he greets.

I could blow this all out of the water right now. But in the same instant I make a decision. I decide to sit it out. I have to go to the bloody play; I'm doing a piece on it for *Way Hey Lady!* magazine. I need time to process my response to Monica, I need time to process how I'll explain this to Declan. I need to work out how I can salvage my dignity, if it's not already beyond saving by me sitting here pretending I didn't hear what I just heard. Monica doesn't bat an eyelid.

'Declan, long time no see. How are you?' she asks.

'I am GOOD.' he announces, bouncing into the banquette alongside me.

'I just switched careers, from advertising to THE ABYSS!' Declan tells her.

'Oh,' she says, both pleased at the diversion and irritated by his manner. She finds him annoying at the best of times.

I mime to the waiter that we'd like another place laid for Declan, and when he comes over I quickly order a salad and a glass of wine and excuse myself. No doubt I'll get the full dramatised and embellished lowdown on Declan's pitch adventure later. I leave Monica to it. I hope he irritates the shit out of her in the exposition. Though, who knows, maybe she'll relish the quality one-to-one with my man friend, seeing as she's obviously been making a habit of it. The ground sways beneath me as I rise.

Chumps is a theatre restaurant, every inch of wall covered by actors' headshots; four hundred sets of eager eyes pleading like dog-pound-puppies. Many of the prints are signed in loose thespian scrawls: 'To Derek, chowder on darling! Dee Dee Doyle xxx,' 'Missed the fudge pud, a tragedy worse than the Scottish play!!!! Ivan P. Steel', that sort of thing. Varied as the faces are, when you've seen one you've seen them all: cheekbones, eyes, desperation, that's about it. I don't want them, or any one in the real world, to see me cry.

I shakily push through the door labelled 'actresses' and lock myself in a cubicle, finally, thankfully, alone. I sit on the closed toilet with my head in my hands. I'd expected a full-on blubber from myself, but now I'm here all that comes is a few stinging tears. 'Think sad,' I tell myself. 'Get the tears out of the system.' Puppies, floods, starving children, Heather Mills-McCartney holding a rabbit fur coat – the mood just won't come. Then I remember something Rory said, the last time we were together. He said, 'you know McNice, when I think about it, you're really special to me.' Now that's worth a few tears. *The soul would have no rainbow had the eyes no tears,* Daddy's voice comes back to me.

I try to see myself in gritty black and white, in a slow revolving overhead shot. The soundtrack is something like 'Cavatina' mournfully plucked on a Spanish guitar. It's working, 'til Mammy comes in and ruins it all:

You shouldn't have got involved with Rory. You shouldn't have allowed it to carry on as long as it did. You would have met someone decent by now. You could have been married and settled. But you were used. You're too trusting. I told you to watch that Monica.

Yes, Mammy. Yes, Mammy, yes, Mammy.

You're just like me.

Yes, Mammy. Yes. I am you. There's no getting away from it. What a disappointment. I should at least have had the decency to grow up and be somebody totally different, someone less like a doormat. Someone like Anita Roddick; do you think she wastes her time trying to blubber in toilets? She does not. She's too busy out in the world sourcing new flavours of make-up, defending endangered crickets and making millions because she knows she's worth it.

'Come on, don't sit here sobbing, McNice,' I tell myself, 'get out there and do something!' I will! I resolve to get pissed as a coot after the play and deal with the whole thing tomorrow. Good plan, Mary. When I finally emerge from the cubicle and look in the mirror, a panda stares back at me. My few dribbly tears have blacked my eyes with smudged mascara. It doesn't matter, actually, I think, the worse-for-wear, slightly-bruised look is in at the moment.

I don't feel like returning to the table, but because of Declan I do. The food has arrived and they're eating.

'... the applause, that was the funniest bit,' he's bellowing through his chow at Monica. 'CAN YOU IMAGINE?'

'Yes,' she answers in a sullen tone that says she's freaked by Declan's weird exuberance and his no doubt unusual tale of work. I would be fully justified in picking up her plate of fish and smattering the whole buttery heap of it all over her hard face as I pass, but I don't. I sit in and eyeball my salad.

'Hope you don't mind, we started without you, Mary,' Declan says. 'I have to say these big sausages are delicious. I love a GOOD BIG SAUSAGE. I love the way the SIZE of the

RESTAURANT sausage has grown in tandem with THE ECONOMY – article idea there for you, my dear. Mary? Are you OK?'

'Yeah, yeah, fine. Just got a touch of hay fever or something. I dunno.' I say, to account for the raw look about me.

'And there was us thinking it was problems in the BOTTOM DEPARTMENT,' he winks at Monica. She winces.

In the normal course of events, Monica would be reminding me that I only have ten minutes to eat, but now, no. The least provocation might set off an exponential reaction. I know she wants to be at the theatre early. It's the opening night and I'm sure she's dying to push her mug in front of whatever hack photographer has turned up there, and lay a quote on any lig-weary press diarist: *Monica Duffy was looking forward to her friend Babette Manion's play: 'I love her work. She's so now.'* I pick at my lettuce on a bed of lettuce or however they pitched it on the menu. I've no appetite. The one upside of trauma – the potential weight lost. Now if only I could feel this bad for another six weeks, I could definitely shift that extra couple of pounds I always carry.

I can't taste the food. I just grind a few mouthfuls of foliage. It goes down like compost, so I give up and swill my wine instead, thinking about Rory. Yes, Rory is of an excellent vintage: firm, full bodied, lingers on the tongue, if a bit bitter in the aftertaste. He's got a nice nose on him, too. In fact, you could say he's fairly first division as men go. And now he's gone. Oh, boo hoo.

'A thirst on you, my dear?' Declan asks.

I inadvertently burp in answer.

'We should be going soon,' Monica says.

Well, Holy God, she just couldn't resist.

She waves to the waiter for the bill. We divvy it up and pay.

Ignited Sambucas come with the change. Monica is sidling out of her seat to leave, ignoring the complimentary digestif. I blow the flame off of mine, wait for it to cool and down it in one. Repeat with Monica's. She's flounced off to get her coat. I watch her struggle into it. It's a lime green, boucle-effect, Nuala MacCool three-quarter length opera coat, loose yet structured, casual yet sophisticated, 100% mixed fibres, yet fifteen hundred euro. She's always well turned out. Is that what attracted Rory to her?

'I like your outfit. Very Diana Dors,' Declan says to me. As we get up to follow Monica, I tell him we can trade tales of woe, later, alone.

'ARE YOU OK?' he asks again.

'Shh,' I tell him, 'later, OK?'

He nods, and pats me a little too hard on the back.

CHAPTER 12

Monica has taken the lead as we proceed in triangular formation to The Project for Babette's premier; down across still busy Dame Street, past the suspended lump of the Central Bank, into the cobbled knot of Temple Bar. Declan is, thankfully, quiet, but even his silence is loud, as if it's just the precursor to another verbal explosion. I deliberately avoid eye contact to preclude that. So there's no chat. Whether Monica and I will ever talk again remains to be seen. Our footfalls on the cobblestones make conversation in our stead. 'In a hurry', 'OK, in a hurry', 'Faster,' 'OK, faster,' 'Onward,' 'Onward', our shoes clip to each other. Wordlessly, we trot past the New York pizza takeaway and the Sinead-O'Connor-worked-here-once-upon-a-time pizza place and across the main piazza.

On the corner, a well-known bespectacled entertainer in a corduroy jacket is providing impromptu amusement for passersby. He has a guitar and an amp and a head-set mic and a strong line in the improvised gag. With his permanently startled look, he has an edginess that suggests he could just as easily wield his guitar as a bludgeon and batter his ad hoc audience to a bloody pulp as delicately strum another amusing tunette from its strings. A clutch of tourists have gathered themselves around him.

'Skinny woman, walking down the street,' he sings, eyeing Monica as she flies past. His audience follow his gaze and Monica becomes the focus of their laughter. He makes some comment about 'one woman's private famine' that I don't quite hear, but I laugh along. 'A minute on the lips, Mary' Monica has always told me. 'Yes,' I used to think to myself as I'd reach for the *Starbar* or dunk the second *Hobnob,* 'But Rory tells me men like hips; men like a bit of padding on The Ladies; men like their squeeze to be squeezy'. 'Come here, you big heifer,' he'd growl in my ear, and I'd just drop my 12-14 tangas and go 'moo'. Now the self-same advocate of the extra potato is cooing, 'come here, Skeletor' to my supposed gal pal. He's stroking bony M, and he's happy? Who were those 'men' Rory was on about? Messrs Liar and Lie-For-A-Shag?

I look up and the street entertainer's audience is still laughing. But now it's at me. 'Welly woman, stumbling down the street/welly woman, missing wellies on her feet ... ' I hear him sing after me. Head down, I hurry away from him as fast as stilettos wobbling on cobble will allow.

The foyer of The Project is buzzing with the opening night crowd. I ask Declan to sort out our tickets with Monica while, pen and notebook in my paw, I forage for pre-show copy to flesh out my *Way Hey Lady!* article. But my head is wrecked with the Rory/Monica information. I mill around, not sure whether I'm recognising 'personalities' or not. Is that puffy guy over there, with the cowboy jacket and the big rings, the doctor who accidentally killed the mother of four with the wrong injection in 'The Surgery'? Is the girl with the pink hair extensions the prostitute who lost her toes in 'Tough Junkies'? Is that chap with the skin condition a director or something? Do I remember him saying he wanted 'to move into film'? What was his name again? Omar? Mark? Rory? Rory, Rory, Rory ...

I spot Babette then, over beside the poster for her play. The poster features a grainy graphic image of naked bodies contorted together in such a way that the focal point is a female face squashed cheek to cheek with a male bottom. I know how that squashed face is feeling. 'Hard-hitting' is what reviewers all think about Babette's work, apparently. The play tonight, *WHACK*, is the final of a trilogy about 'modern relationships', I read this off the flyer as I make my way over to her. The other two, *SLAM* and *THRASH*, were big hits on the fringe everywhere, or so the puff says. She's momentarily alone as I reach her. Great, quick question, quick answer, that'll do me.

'Congratulations, Babette, the last of the trilogy?'

'Yes,' she answers. 'But what are you doing with the notebook? I thought you worked in television?'

'Oh, I did. Now I do this. I'm doing a rev... erm, a *piece* on your play. I've got a weekly column too. Don't know if you've seen it?'

'No. No, don't think I have.'

Babette's been away in England, of course, on a scholarship, doing an M.A. in Modern Punchy Theatre or something. She wouldn't know ...

'Yeah, I left telly to concentrate on the journalism.'

'Lovely,' Babette says.

'Look, I don't want to hold you up. Can I just ask you a few quick questions: How does it feel to be back in Dublin, opening your first play since you got back? How do you feel right now before the curtain goes up? The play is about relationships – are you in a relationship at the moment?' The questions tumble out and run into one another. I don't care; wring anything out of her, it'll do. I don't want to have to talk to anyone else. There's a pause while she absorbs what I've asked. 'How's it all going?' I add, determined to get something out of her.

There's a beat. Finally she says, 'I love being back in Dublin, I love working here, I feel nervous but positive right now, and if you must know, I *am* in a relationship, in love and things are going well, thanks. I've got to go.'

She turns to another first-night well-wisher. I resist the temptation to ask, who? Who are you in the relationship with – Name? Status? Is he a hunk? Or is he a she? *Way Hey Lady* magazine likes the social and personal angle on everything. 'Thanks a million,' I tell Babette's back and I note down: ♥Dub, ♥wking here, nervous but ☺, in relationship, in♥, things ☺ – Babette Manion. That'll be grand. Lolly Lynham, the editor, loved my colonic irrigation piece, I'm sure I can bum my way through this commission too.

'Come on,' Declan says, 'let us be seated.'

People are queuing to enter the auditorium. I note Monica going in ahead of us. Good. I couldn't bear to sit next her through *WHACK*. I'd be afraid I'd take the play's title as a suggested response to her shocking betrayal.

But my relief is shortlived. As soon as we're in the theatre, there's Monica waving us to two spaces she has saved, beside her. Before I have time to react, Declan is moving toward her. I cannot but follow. People at the end of the row rise to allow us pass, and Declan, ever the gentlemen, lets me precede him. So I end up sitting beside Monica. I cannot bear to look at her. I angle my body away from her, tensing lest we touch. Declan leans across me to say thanks for keeping the seats, squashing me toward her. I lean forward out of the friendly pincer to rummage in my handbag. I have to find my phone, turn it off. I pull it out and there are seven new messages. My first reaction is a heart-flipping 'oops, what's happened'; my second, on viewing the first message, is, oh, oh, oh, oh, oh …

GR8 4 U – N1!

Mrs. 2B, congr8s!

So Ding Dong Ur Bells R Gg to ring!

3iffic! Hope he 6Y motherF!

Etcetera, etcetera, etcetera. Just GR8.

The last is from Breege:

Saw u on tv - Wht a srprse! U nvr said 2day! Still in hspt– btm stitches. Hope 2 be relesd 2moro. Thks for coming in u are a pal X. PS. Is it Rory?

Is it Rory? Isn't it always, I think, as the auditorium lights go down and I switch off the phone.

The lights come up on the stage. There's a man there, staring out at the audience.

'Poor prick,' Declan whispers to me, 'he's probably wondering if everyone's ogling his knob.'

The man is naked.

'See, you're not the only one with a demanding job,' I retort.

'Shh,' someone shushes us from behind. The least a seriously naked actor deserves is a bit of hush. The audience holds its breath, reverentially tense. I'm tense with my proximity to The Traitor. Then a woman joins the man and she's naked too, except for glasses. Thankfully, The Traitor crosses her legs away from me and I cross my legs too, so there's a big 'V' of space between us.

NUDE MAN: Her hair. Long. Red. Eyes, green. Short. Sighted. Or long. She's interested?'

NUDE WOMAN: Him. The hard old scar on the cheek, that I'd love to lick and I don't know why. Him, his thick hair, his thick lips, the thick look about him and that thinking look in the eye that rolls over you like a punch. Interesting?

NUDE MAN: Her breasts…

Please be over soon, I will the show.

Man and woman circle each other, and that turns into a sort of dance, to a piece of music that sounds like a hungry cat accompanied by a dustbin. On stage they're dressing. Then they talk about whether or not they will ever really know each other as they get to know each other over the next one hour and twenty minutes straight through, no intermission.

What's really true? That's one of the questions Babette is posing in *WHACK*. There's no doubt about her intention, because it's projected in huge black letters on the white cyc. at the back of the stage. WHAT'S REALLY TRUE?

By the same manner we also know Babette is getting at TRUST? FIDELITY? HOW DO YOU KNOW? INTIMACY? and then just LOVE? flashed very quickly, creating a strobe effect as the protagonists undress again, towards sex, possibly, or some such inevitability.

Suddenly it all screeches to a halt. The screen blanks, the music cuts. The female has found a gun in the man's cast-aside trousers. Slowly and surprised, she looks at the gun, slowly and horrified, she looks at the audience, slowly she turns to the man. Quickly she cocks, aims and shoots him. The actor does a good fall. The lights cut except for a **?** pulsating on the backdrop.

Then blackout. There's a moment's hesitancy from the audience, then the stutter of building applause. It reaches its crescendo as the actors appear on stage in dressing gowns. They bow, and whoops and cheers supplement the hand clapping. The End.

Declan limply pats his programme on his knee – his contribution to the appreciative din.

'Thanks,' he says to me, 'thanks for bringing me to that. Interesting – a cross between a clip show and torture. Now, can we quick step it across the road, I could really *WHACK* a pint.'

I force a laugh, hoping I won't have to do the polite thing with Monica. I don't want to speak to her. Luckily, she spots an acquaintance in the row behind and swivels her body anti-clockwise away from me, as they get stuck into a conversation about how powerful the piece was: how devastating is the whole idea of do we ever really know, can we ever really trust, another human being? I want to turn around and say, 'actually, Monica has the capacity to deliver a much more devastating *WHACK* than anything we saw on stage tonight.' But I don't. Thankful that she's otherwise engaged, I hurry after Declan to the door. On the way out, I hear someone say that the play is based on a true story. Wow.

Outside in the foyer, Declan gets waylaid by a glass of wine.

'Just the one,' he promises. He knows I want to go.

'When I get back from the loo ... ' I give him his drink time-limit.

Of course, when I return I see him reaching for the second

glass. I'm moving toward him, oblivious to all else. In the press of people I bang shoulders with a woman. She turns. It's Monica and we're face to face. Some word ought to pass between us, but there's nothing. We stare at each other. I fleetingly notice she's starting to get grey hairs. We're frozen; we need a word to break the spell, but I cannot …

'Look,' she says after what seems like the proverbial forever.

'I'd rather not,' I say, turning sharply from her and moving toward the exit. My heart is pounding, I'm trembling, I bump violently into a man right behind me.

'Ach, fuckit, me shirt,' he says.

I've sent a glass of red wine all over a man's nice white shirt. I stare at the widening wet slash of red on his chest, matching the deepening bloom of his face. It's the eczema/possibly director fella from before, I realise. Whatever it is that he does, the fact that he's known as a prima donna rings a rumour bell in my head.

'Jesus. Sorry,' I blurt out.

'Blast it,' he says, as someone rushes to his aid with a fistful of napkins to dab the damage. He looks at his shirt, he looks at me, his face seems to glow brighter, like an alarm. He's making a scene. People are watching. He is raging. I'm speechless. What can I say?

'There might be a spare shirt in wardrobe,' a venue-person offers super-urgently, as if she's offering him a tourniquet for the bleeding stump of a recently blown-off limb.

'For fecks sake,' I say to both of them, 'it's only a drop of wine.'

They look at me as if I'm Peter having just triple denied the soon-to-be-dead Christ. Jesus. I have to get out of here. I push through the post-show throng, through the foyer and escape into the street.

I'm glad of the sharp, cold air outside. It hits me like a slap, bringing me to my senses, and making me want to cry, but I don't. There's a cumulus of post-show smokers gathering next to me. Declan comes tumbling through the heavy doors, anxious in my wake, drink still in hand.

'Jesus, what's going on with you? Did you throw a glass of wine at the guy, or something?'

'No. The feckin' eejit. No.'

'Well, that's what it kind of looked like.'

'Oh, God.'

'What happened then?'

'Can I tell you what's *really* happened?'

He lights me and himself a fag, even though I don't officially smoke. We stand in the cold, sucking on our cigarettes, exhaling blue veils about ourselves.

'This is about Monica, isn't it?' he asks.

'Yeah,' I confirm, 'it's about Monica. And Rory.'

Declan looks suitably surprised. I spill my story into the greasy, hop-smelling air of the dark Dublin night.

He shakes his head silently when I'm finished.

'Well, I consider myself fairly well versed in all the variegations of human nature, but that, I agree, takes the Kimberley.'

'Yeah, what a surprise Monica turned out to be, after fifteen years,' I add.

'Hey, it takes two to TANGO, Mary,' he admonishes me.

'Look, I know you never liked Rory ... ' I say

'And was I right or was I RIGHT?'

'I can't say, Declan, but I don't need a sermon now. I need to know the details, I have to know the details.'

'What? LIKE WHERE, WHEN, HOW MANY TIMES AND IN

WHAT POSITION? OR POSITIONS?'

'Declan, please don't rub it in, don't say stuff like that now. Please, it's not what I need to hear ... ' my voice is about to give way to tears.

He hugs me with his free arm and apologises.

'Sorry, SORRY, but sometimes I just wanted to SHAKE you for being involved with that PRICK. Maybe now you've woken up to what he is.'

'Yeah, but what about Monica in all of this, maybe I've just woken up to her?' I say, pulling away from him.

'Yeah, yeah, sure, it's all Monica's fault.'

We're at a stand-off. Declan breaks it by scrubbing my arm with his free hand. 'Look, I don't want to get bolshie with you. What's happened is awful for you, full stop. Period. Let me buy you a fancy drink across the road and cheer you up. OK?'

'OK,' I agree, 'and you can tell me what went on with you today.' I know there's no point having this out with Declan. How can I explain to him what I felt, what I still feel, with regard to Rory? It defies logic, there's no talking it out with anyone other than ...

'OK, if you insist, my dear. Let's see how we both bear up under all the high drama,' he lightens his tone, 'one minute and I'll be back.'

As he goes inside to return his glass and do whatever he needs to, I switch my phone back on. There's one new message. From Rory:

Where R U?

Yes, of course I feel like not replying, but it's impolite not to get back.

NOYB I text. There, I'm getting assertive and I'll have many an extra letter to add in person. He won't be expecting me to show up anywhere near him tonight now. But I will. Oh boy, I will. I'm sick of being … of being the kind of person that this kind of thing can happen to. Isn't that what it's really all about? He's going to get an earful from me if it's the last thing he gets.

'A McNice COCKTAIL so?' Declan asks, re-emerging.

I nod and we go across the road to The Clarence.

CHAPTER 13

We're in the snug of The Clarence. We've the door closed, shutting out the rest of the bar. We could almost be in the past, and we would be if they were selling tea, sandwiches and Tayto with warm pints of Guinness out there, and there was a live fire dancing in the grate, and a granny's parlour carpet on the floor. And if you went out and were meeting up with people coming to or from England or New York or wherever the work was. It certainly wasn't in Dublin back then – but oh, I'm going way way back thinking about that: over a decade ago. I remember Breege, Monica and I hooking up in here, Monica in from NY, me from London, Breege from Ranelagh. We're the transition generation; we've seen both sides: The Nothing and The Everything.

We've seen The Rock Stars bounce in here in their leather pants with the deep pockets, booting out the old upholstery, the real flames, the mad staff and the past, and putting up the weird lighting and the giant vases and the prices. We've seen the future and it's now. When just going for a pint in an old haunt tests the stretch of your memories like this, that's what's called getting older, I believe ...

'Mary, are you listening to me?' Declan asks.

'I just had a flashback to what it used to be like here,' I tell him.

'Yeah. Yeah, that's lovely, granny. But do you want to hear this or not?'

'Sorry, sorry. Yeah, where were you?'

Right,' Declan says.'I was in the conference room of O'C, O'C, O'D & Y, if you'd like to come back with me to this afternoon.'

I nod and sip my cocktail. The strong alcohol is eroding the shock of earlier revelations.

'Picture the scene: suits assembled around top-of-the-range Danish table. To my right, client manager, to my left art director, in the centre, moi, GOD. Naturellement. Client manager moistens lips with Evian and begins. The Intro: pithy and anxious to clinch this massive account, and POSITIVE that we will because of the BRILLIANCE of ME. Then over to me. Expectant silence. I arise and begin. "*COME AND GET IT*" MY IDEA totally, remember? They're liking it; I want them to love it. And I know I can make them because – I don't know if I told you before, Mary – but I am VERY good at my job.'

'*Was* very good at your job, from what you've told me. *Was*,' I interject.

'*WAS*, whatever. Anyway. Rex, on art, illustrates all angles with OUR great mock-ups. And he's good, nearly as good as me, as I *was*, even if he is a knob-head. Anyway, I launch into the clincher, the *COME AND GET IT* – not just a product name, but a call to arms, a drop-everything mantra to NEED the chocolate immediately. Surgeons drop the scalpel mid by-pass, father leaves the splayed legs of his beloved as the baba's just coming, blah, blah, you get the picture. And all because the fella loves good chocolate. I'm giving it good-o, acting all the parts and doing the SFX. And then, and I don't know where this came from, but to illustrate I go into the "Come and Get It" trance I'm describing. AND THEY BUY IT! Silence, focus, you can almost hear their breath, their heartbeats. I've got them! I just stand there – stock-still, staring out the window, into the sky – for, I dunno, thirty, sixty, ninety or more seconds?'

Declan pauses, remembering.

'You're doing it again,' I tell him.

'And that's when I had the epiphany,' he continues, slower.

'The epiphany?'

'Yeah. I'm just standing there and there's this amazing parallax thing going on with the clouds: layers of mist shifting over each other at different speeds, really fast, and almost still at the same time, fast and still and the sky-blue opening and closing between the overlap and … and I just walked out.'

'You just walked out of the meeting?'

'Yeah. And the funny thing is, as I headed down the hall, I heard them break into spontaneous applause. Sustained. As if I'd left to *COME AND GET IT* and I'd be back in a jiffy, munching chocolate. They were waiting for me! I just packed my desk and left.'

'Wow.'

'I'm sure we got the account, but I'm out. Out. It's over.'

'You think? Don't you think what you did will probably just be seen as eccentric but, in your own word, BRILLIANT. If you have won the account I'm sure everybody's happy and you'll be back in the fold Monday morning.'

'Oh, I forgot to add that on the way out I made a detour to Crispin's office and scrawled 'ARSE HOLE' in red marker all over the available paper on his desk.'

'Who's Crispin?'

'The client manager. My overlord, in other words.'

'Oh. Right. So you *are* gone.'

'Yep, and there's no going back.'

'Why did you do that?'

'So there would be no going back.'

'OK ... '

'I heard the applause dribble to a stop. But I'm sure Crispin managed my desertion with panache. PANACHE, that's Crisp in a word. '

'Right, but all a bit potty, no?'

He shrugs, we silently clink our glasses and drink.

'And now?' I ask.

'And *now* I'm having a drink here with you.'

'No, the *bigger* now – as in tomorrow?'

He shrugs.

'Erm, the travel writing,' I remind him.

'Nah. If I mentioned that before, I wasn't serious. The last thing the world needs is another middle class WHITEY in retro sand shoes tripping THE ROUGH FANTASTIC in less fortunate time zones.'

'You don't have to rough it, what about all the junkets? What about those fab holidays you read about in Sunday Supplements – you know, 'the reporter flew first class on Hog Heaven Airlines, and spent five nights in the seven star Your-Wish-Is-Our-Command Compound. In fact, I want you to *be* a travel writer, Declan. And I want to come too. I could be the anonymous friend who tried and enjoyed the seven-hour relaxing massage, while you had a snorkelling lesson and a pedicure. I can help you find the adjectives for the *crisp* bed linen and the *yummy* lobster and the *really big hot* sun, you know what I mean, I really like the idea.'

'Yes, McGreedy but no, McGreedy.'

'And think of all the weekend hops – we'd never be at a loose end again – staying in a boutique hotel here one weekend, a B&B made of ice there the next. I'm not totally joking, you know.'

'Yeah, methinks all those Sunday Supplement you're reading are English. I think the reality in Ireland is a little more low-fi. Long weekends in TRABOLGAN, more like.'

'Oh. Well. So what were you thinking?'

'Third-World. Volunteer. Help. I haven't worked it out yet; I just have the key words. But that is what I am thinking, if you must know. That is what I am going to do.'

Great.

'Right, so not only are you robbing me of my holiers, you're also leaving me. Thanks.'

Just great.

'No, I don't know. Maybe. I haven't looked into it in detail, Mary, I'm just saying. But I feel I should do something with my life. While I can. Open the aperture. Look at the bigger picture. I'm serious.'

'Yeah,' I whisper.

My own picture is shrinking. Where before there was me and three bosom pals and a lover, now there's just me with Declan (going away), Monica (finished), Rory (over), and Breege – baby, husband, different planet. Despite myself, I feel tears prickling my eyes.

'You're not crying, are you?' Declan asks.

'No,' I cry.

'Ah,' he says, putting his arm around me. 'I'm really touched that you'd cry over me leaving.'

He roots in my handbag, finds some tissue and dabs my eyes. I wish there was something big I could say right now that would take the fear out of what I'm feeling. Something like, 'I love you'. And then in *True Romance Reality* Declan would reply: 'I love you too', and we'd both be shocked by the obviousness of it and be instantly transformed into Mr & Mrs Right-For-Each-Other. And the new departure in his life wouldn't be a one-way to Addis Ababa, but a trip up the aisle to me in the meringue dress. And his Bigger Picture wouldn't be Africa but the group shot on the opening page of our wedding album. And that ring on my finger would be rest-of-your-life insurance against this sickening pang of emptiness.

But that's not about to happen. Declan and I are no more attracted to each other than a cow to a horse. We both know that. It's the most basic tenet of our friendship. Unspoken, but we're both absolutely clear about it. So, to cheer myself, I'm able to tell him what just crossed my mind.

We both laugh about it. 'That sort of scenario is not total fantasy though,' I say, 'I've heard it happen for people our age. Mid-thirties, end of the youth age bracket – feel you have to settle down ... '

'Settle for something ... '

'Anything. Yeah.'

We're silent for a while.

'All that apart, you know what? I do bloody love you, Declan Twomey,' I say with an affectionate smile, patting his knee.

'And it goes without saying that I love you too, you BIG MCNICE,' he answers.

In the normal course of events, he might have patted me on the knee, too. But his arm is still around my shoulder so he just pulls me closer to him and we're filled with the warmth of our platonic connection. With so much warmth, in fact, that almost of their own volition, our mouths meet, our lips part, and our arms fold about each other. We're not so much embracing as clinging.

And that's how we end up snogging in the snug of The Clarence.

CHAPTER 14

I'm in a toilet cubicle, upstairs. 'Well, I'm definitely heading to The Madra Rua later, whatever you guys are up to. OK?' I hear Monica's voice outside the door.

She's just come in with some of Babette's gang, the *SLAM, BAM, WHACK* brigade, or whatever the name of all the plays were. One, two, three cubicle doors slam bam shut. I don't want to hear any more; don't want to see her; have to meet her. And I certainly don't want her to know that I may have just overheard what I heard – *The Madra Rua* later, is it? What a coincidence, that's exactly where I'm headed. And we both know why.

Dec and I have to get out of here quick sharp, that's all I know. I'm two strong cocktails to the wind and it's all as clear as Cosmopolitans to me. I'm out of the stall in two seconds flat, clattering down the stairs and into Declan in the snug before I have time to let logic catch up with me:

'Go,' I say. 'We. Now.'

He looks at me over his pint.

'WHY, pray tell, oh one of the FLUSHED demeanour?' He asks.

'Monica. Upstairs. Now. We. Before.' He'll have to fill in the verbs and other stuff himself. I'm pulling on my coat, and then draining the last of my €13 bevvy. Despite my hurry, I manage to take a moment to give the straw a good poke around the latent ice, and make sure every last drop has been hoovered.

Declan swallows the rest of his Guinness without urgency. It's no bother to him, when he's really drinking he can make a pint look like a thimbleful. Of lemonade. This one is his third since we sat down.

'Yeah, I saw her when I went to the bar.'

'And, and, and?' I ask.

'AND what?'

'I dunno,' I answer. 'Come.'

He follows me to the door. We're out without having seen Monica again.

'Phew!' I say.

'Drama queen,' is his only comment, as he links my arm and we head toward Westmorland Street. Down through the main drag of Temple Bar, through the street-spill of smokers, revellers and muzak, past bars chock-a-block with bunny-eared hens, legless dancers, hammered stags – into the essence of Friday night. Declan is inspired, or pissed – same difference in this vibe.

'REGARD this buzzing Dublin BAZAAR of booze and loosened people. May I interest you in a jewel of Tequila, a carpet of Puke or a ... OOPS A DAISY! ... or a bride-to-be of some unfortunate Scouse Godzilla.' A woman almost comes a cropper in front of us. Her veil falls off, and, in one inebriated move, she manages to pick it up and jam it back on her head, all the while keeping balance with her spare hand splayed on the ground. She's wearing a very short skirt. We watch her knickers.

'SNATCH I think is the word,' Declan comments.

'*The Star* is missing a front page here,' I quip.

'Owww, me fucking foot's fucked,' she shouts to her brood of chums ahead in the street.

They turn and come clucking back to her aid.

'Ahhh, chuck ... '

There's an 'L' plate pinned to her back.

'Makes it look like she's a learner walker,' I comment.

'Yeah, and here's her stabilisers,' Declan adds, as each of her arms is clamped in the firm grip of a supportive girlfriend.

'Onwards from this FOWL SCENE,' Declan says grandiosely, doing his best Oscar Wilde impression. We stumble off.

We feel like a couple. This is what I've always really wanted with Rory, the easy companionship, but R. and I never seem to hang out enough to allow that happen. Now that we're chugging along a bit slower, I apologise to Declan for rushing him out of The Clarence. 'It was stupid, I know. I suppose I just didn't want her to think we'd be in The Madra Rua later.'

'Which we won't be,' Declan says.

'Oh. I was really hoping, I'd planned in my head that–'

'No,' Declan says, unlinking my arm.

'Please, please, *please,* come with me, Declan. Please.'

I can't get in without Declan. He probably knows that.

'I hate that KIP. That jumped up WATERING HOLE for jungle scum. Why do you want to go there of all places?' he asks.

'Because ... '

'Because Rory will be there,' he answers for me.

'Yeah. OK. You're right. Because Rory will be there. Sorry.'

'Don't sorry me, Mary, sorry yourself. That after all this SHITE you're still running after him.' Declan has stopped walking and is facing me.

'I'm not ...'

'You are. Have you no DIGNITY?'

'I just want ... '

'Yeah?'

'Closure.'

'Oh. OH. Would you listen to OPRAH WINFREY. *Closure*. Since when did IRISH PEOPLE start looking at life like it's doors you can open and *CLOSURE*? JESUS, leave the IMBECILIC OUTLOOK to Imperial Kiddieland across the pond.'

His anger has flared from nowhere. Jaysus, he'll be blaming me for the war in Iraq in a minute.

'What's wrong with you, Declan? What *is* wrong?' If he can do the anger thing so can I. 'Can't you allow me this small satisfaction. I have to see Rory tonight. I have to let him know ... '

'If there's anything you want to let him know, let him know by having absolutely NO contact with him ever again,' he shouts.

'What does it matter to you, why are you getting so over the top about this?' I shout back. God, I hate this.

'Because I AM YOUR FRIEND. WE ARE FRIENDS. FRIENDS!!! I thought we just made that clear to each other.'

That comment brings our exchange to a grinding halt. To fill the awful silence, we start ambling forward again. Glumly.

'I just HATE to see you make a doormat of yourself. And that's what you are doing,' he says eventually, quieter.

It's the kiss, I'm thinking. We started snogging and then we stopped and that was it. I laughed and commented that I suppose we had to get that out of the way at some point, even if it was years in. And he instantly nodded his accord, got up to get more drinks, and when he came back it was grand again.

Maybe the drink was to cloak the naked embarrassment? But honestly there just isn't that *thing,* that *zing* between us. It would be so easy if there were, but there just isn't – never has been. I'm just grateful more drink hadn't been taken up 'til The Meeting of The Mouths. Jesus, can you imagine, we could so easily have ended up in my bed: waking in the brittle morning, uncomfortably naked under the duvet, uncomfortably aware of too much contact the night before and two hangovers ripping the heads off us, and that awful 'oh no' feeling enveloping the whole situation. And then trying to normalise everything with rasher sandwiches and Solpadeine.

'That's just what I think,' he says.

'What?'

'You're being a DOORMAT.'

'Oh.'

I should tell him I come from a long and honourable line of female doormats. But I don't. I apologise instead, another inherited tick.

'I'm sorry. I'm sorry.' I tell him twice, for good measure. Even though I don't honestly know *what* it is I am apologising for.

'OK,' he accepts. I take his arm again, as we walk.

We're at the foot of Grafton Street. We need to make our decisions.

'Look, Declan,' I plead, 'As a friend, I'm telling you I need to see Rory tonight, and *as a friend* I'm asking you to *please* come with me. Because I can't get into The Madra Rua without you, to be totally honest.'

The Madra Rua is a private members club, a celebrity haunt. Declan has membership by default, through his work. You've to either have membership or be 'known' to get in. I don't have the former, and whenever I've tried to sidle my way in with an attempted 'you must know who I am!' attitude, Jockser, the owner, has always stopped me and asked 'who are you?'

'Do you think I don't know that? That I hadn't thought of that? You may have noticed we're headed in the direction of The Madra Rua, that we're nearly there and that that's not *entirely* ACCIDENTAL,' Declan says. I take it he's saying 'yes'. Yes, we are going to the club.

'Thanks, Declan, you're a friend,' I acknowledge.

'I know,' he replies flatly.

It's too early to go straight there. We decide to pop into another den of inebriation on the way. 'It'll be thronged,' he says, 'but fuck it. DRINK. FECK. ARSE.'

CHAPTER 15

'... ah yeah, right, it's so true about men, and ya know the way it is – it really is, ya know what I mean? Yer man was right. It really is. That's what I thought anyway, very good, must get that book, what was it called again?'

'*Trash the Pants.*'

'*Trash the Pants, Trash the Pants,* yeah, yeah.'

'Well, thanks very much,' I say, not sure what it is I'm thanking her for, for 'recognising' me perhaps? Mainly, I'm just hoping the 'thanks' will be the end of my 'conversation' with this young wan, who 'saw me on de telly and had to come over and tell me'. It's not *Trash the Pants* she needs, something more like *Wear Some Clothes, How To.* She's kitted out in what looks like a sequinned hanky. It barely covers her ... anything. Her friends ditto: they all look like they've walked off the pages of *NUTS* magazine. They're obviously up for it, but I'd imagine your Mr Average is totally intimidated by them. I'd imagine he prefers that look where he can handle it – between his sticky paws, on the glossy page that was his to take home for €2.50. Then again, maybe these girls aren't out to pull your Mr Average. They're 'aspiring'. It's the times. Poor men.

Anyway, I didn't expect to be recognised, it's a bit weird.

'And best of luck yourself,' she says, with a smile and an encouraging dig on my arm. ' ... and I like the skirt, it looks good on ya. Me ma has one li ...' and, thankfully, she's together enough to stop herself right there. She totters off on her implausible heels.

'Did you not see the bit at the end of the interview?' I should call after her, 'where I revealed that I am engaged!!! I am *engaged,* did you not get that – although it looks like it, I am *not* alone. I may be wearing a skirt, but get this – I don't need to! I could be standing here in a potato sack! Hair full of slurry! It doesn't matter because I've already Bagged. A. Man. Did you not hear that bit today?'

But I don't. I wave her off, faking nonchalance, quietly para-noid now that everyone recognises me just as she did, and none of them recall my engagement announcement: 'Yeah, the spinster from the telly – there she is, alone on a Friday night, waiting for some weekend-dregs of a fella to fall into the trap of her big skirt. Tsk, tsk, sad, isn't it.' Please come back right now, I silently will Declan, I need my fiancé 'beard'.

I'm standing beside a big, Parisian *fin du siècle* sideboard, under a piece of potted jungle, in the home of the humongous knick-knack: Café Insane. The last I saw of Declan he had disappeared behind a jumbo urn on his way to the bog, and anything could have happened to him along the way. He could have been flattened under a falling house-sized mirror, or been felled by a monstrous velvet pouffe, or merely eaten alive by a man-hungry gang of half-nudie young nutters.

Or ... dunno ... I'm nursing a vodka Red Bull, Declan's choice. This is my second V&RB; I'll be facing the floor before I face Rory if I'm not careful.

I see him. Declan is staggering back, pushing his way through the braying throng. Jesus, am I as gone as that, I think, looking at him move. It's hard to know these things, particularly with what we've been drinking – the buzz of the Red Bull works totally against the alcohol so that sometimes you can't quite judge if you've had too much until you just suddenly fall over and die. Or so it's been said. Maybe that's just an urban myth ...

'Story?' he says. Yep, he's drunk. When he starts doing his 'Dub' thing.

'Ready to head?' I reply.

'Let's rock 'n' roll but, just so you know, work might be there. My work, you know? Just so you know.'

'What, you're telling me "no". Again?' I ask him.

'No, just telling you.'

He walks on. I skip after him out the door, along to the club, to Rory. I distract him with a lowdown on 'Afternoon Stew' today.

'... and then I found out I wasn't on alone, it was a discussion, a debate, with Kian O'Kelly, you know him?'

'Yeah, yeah.'

'The journo who dumped me in it before ... '

'Yeah, yeah, one of the big boozy uglies.'

'One of them.'

'I know the feeling.'

'Hey, come on, Declan, don't be down on yourself, why the long face–'

'–said the barman to the horse.'

I ignore the negative vibes and continue. I tell him how it all ended in my fib. I'm trying to cheer him, but he explodes.

'So, on top of everything, anyone who saw it and knows you probably thinks you're engaged to the WANKERFUCKERPRICK we're coming here for you to see!'

There's nothing I can say to that, but, thankfully, we're at the door of The Madra Rua. And we are going in. I hope.

CHAPTER 16

A short man in a long coat is on the door. It's Jockser Hunt, the owner. He's backed up by a little herd of beefy bouncers. They stand in formation. You can imagine them practising the pose, ensemble, in front of a dance mirror, in leotards; Jockser directing: 'shoulders back, lads, hands joined over the bollix, look thick, and don't mind me, I'm the leader; I can do any position I fancy. It's my prerogative.'

'Howaya, boss,' Declan greets The Man. The phraseology doesn't suit Declan's slightly grand accent. Jockser takes a beat, flexing his black-leather-gloved hands, maybe thinking Declan is taking the piss, maybe just recognising the fact that we are not the most sober? But then, who is at this time of night, in Dublin, on a Friday? He gives the nod and up we go.

We are in, in with the 'in' crowd. Of sorts. The Madra Rua, Irish, means The Fox. Apt name that; you'd need to be one to be able to see clearly in this place. The walls are deep brown wood veneer, everything else is black. It's incredibly dark; the only variation is the slated mirror that runs the length of the wall behind the long bar, and the mirrored corner of the miniscule dancefloor. Dracula could drink here daytime, no bother. Dracula and a bunch of foxes.

Declan and I stand just inside the door for a moment, acclima-
tising. It's mad noisy.

'Where do you want to stand?' I shout to him. There's nowhere
to sit down. Everyone is on their feet, drinking, chatting, tripping
to the loo and back and half-eyeing the sofas, which look gorgeous in a 'it'd be nice to sit down' kinda way. But they're all out
of bounds, RESERVED, in case any proper VIPS show up, like
Darren O'Marra or anyone who's big on the Telly.

'GARGLE,' Declan declares. 'I'll
find you when I get the drink
in.' He gets stuck into the task.
There's a four deep mob josh-
ing at the bar. You'd swear the
drink was free by the looks of it.
The double-priced opposite is
the truth. Declan will be a while,
but I'm hardly going to get lost. The place is tiny, and jammers,
and the empty sofas seem to take up most of the room, so there's
nowhere to go, really. All the better for me, because I am on a
mission.

'Mission. Mission. Mission.' I repeat that to myself in a childish
chant as I squash through the room, scanning for Rory. Does that
mean I'm quite drunk? Yes. Mission. Does that mean I shouldn't
be here? Yes. Mission. Does that stop me? No. Mission. He's not
there, and he's not over there, but hey! there's Paddy Finn. With a
girl. With whom he's making hand-to-arse contact. But don't jump
to conclusions, Mary with-your-journo-cap-on, maybe it's his wife.
But it can't be. He said his wife was due soon, so unless she's
about to give birth to a prawn, I'd say that stick with a head he's
now wearing the face off is *someone else*. Alas, I'm not looking for

someone else's cheat. I'm looking for my own.

Rory.

He's not in that corner, and he's not talking to him, or to her, or to them, he's not …

I see him.

RORY.

What is it about some people you get attracted to? What imbues them with that power that pulls you to them, like you're a thick cat and they're catnip? What makes the atmosphere ignite when you see them, when you sense they're near? What is it that makes their presence like the pulse thumping in your veins? That makes a glance from them heart-stopping? That makes the possibility of their touch as intense as if it could start your stopped heart again? Oh God, not an ounce of that has gone away. He's every ride you ever wanted rolled into one. You're looking at him and you hear Robbie Williams sing-a-telling you *He's The One … If there's some-body calling me on …*

RORY.

I feel the same. What am I going to say now? 'Hello Rory, you've devastated me. You've been sleeping with someone else the whole time we've been together. You've denied the truth of our connection; the lover's trust I placed in you; the private gospel of our love. Yes, you heard me right. No, I don't think I'm being over-dramatic. You've betrayed me most heinously. And to top it all, you've been seeing one of my friends. And you didn't tell me. I had to find out. You've been sleeping with both of us. The three of us! At the same time. That is shocking. So, would you like to come home with me right now, do it to me one more time 'til dawn and then cuddle up for a few hours, and then maybe we could go out somewhere for brunch in the late am and talk about it? Maybe we could go for a walk on Howth Hill after? Have a few pints and see if we can't work something out in the longer term? If you're free, that is. By the way, I'm wearing the knickers you like … ' Oh Lord, isn't that the real reason I came here this evening?

He sees me and he's getting up. Yes, Rory can even *sit* in this club, he's that special. Here he comes, the tousled hair, the open-necked shirt, the toptastic jacket, the debonaire smirk. One of his phrases, 'hey, what's not to like', seeps into my head as he sidles over by my side – the perfect height above me, as always. 'You *can* have everything,' that's another Rory motto.

Switch to B&W, there's a ripple of piano; in a creamy tenor I never knew he had, he sings, *'It had to be you, it had to be you, I wandered around and finally found …'* As he pulls me into a waltz, everyone looks around, beaming with the kind of benign goodwill that went out of fashion in the late 50s. He puts his sweet lips to my ear.

In reality, he just says, 'hey what's up? What was with the snippy text?'

His hand lightly touches my elbow. I pull away, after a second.

He loses the smile, points to a corner and we sit. He's wearing his 'I'm concerned' look, a sort of George Clooney 'I'm-worried-about-American's-involvement-in-Iraq-and-simultaneously-burdened-by-the-fact-that-everyone-wants-to-shag-me' creasing of the brow. He's giving nothing away.

He says, 'what?'

I say, 'you know what'

He asks, 'do I?'

I say, 'you do.'

Then, in my dreams, he says, *'God, Mary. Mary, forgive me, I've made a terrible mistake.'* Sudden violins saw to a precipitous crescendo, he plants his mouth on mine and crushes my body to his in the manner of a homecoming WWII G.I. ...

In the here and now, he's just repeating, 'I do?'

Maybe he doesn't? Maybe he doesn't know I know anything?

'Yes, you fucking do,' I say.

'Hey, OK, OK. I've heard you've announced our engagement. What do you want me to say?'

I know what I want him to say: *'Yes, yipee!'* while *'FIN'* appears over us in flowery lettering.

'I mean, how *weird*, you know?' he says.

'Yeah, weird for who? Isobel sitting at home, watching the box this afternoon?'

'What? You said it on *televison?* Jesus Christ, Mary, what kind of a–'

'I didn't say *we* were engaged, I pretended *I* was, for technical reasons. Sorry if Isobel was having kittens ...' But it's not my old bête noir Isobel I'm thinking of. I'm waiting for him to mention the M-word.

He doesn't. He says, 'Isobel is out of the picture.'

Isobel. Is. Out. Of. The. Picture.

'Wow,' I say. Somehow the fact that Isobel was married, with kids, to *his* friend, was my reassurance that in time they would end. Then Rory and I would finally skip off through the meadow of commitment together, towards the sunset of basic-unit-of-society. Neither of us was ever quite ready, that was all. That was the grand conclusion I had come to. But it took Monica to make it happen. Monica. M.O.N.I.C.Arrrgghhh! I've been shoved in the ditch along with Isobel. He's not going to say it. I will.

'Monica,' I cry.

He's on damage limitation now.

'OK,' he admits.

He gives me a moment to heave and weep while I take in that admission. The ice cream has finally fallen from the cone, it's melting in the sand, it's gone.

'I don't know how it happened,' he offers softly.

'What? Are you looking to me for the answer? Let me guess, your pants fell around your ankles by their own volition and you just fell into Monica,' I sniff angrily.

'It's not like that.'

'What's it like, then? What's it like? I can tell you what it's like for me if you'd like ... I loved you. I really, really, really fucking did. I. I. I ... lo ... '

But I cannot say it again – the l-word – it's blocked by the images that come up: *I'm kissing him the first time; I'm in bed waking up with him, lying in an intimate tangle of resting limbs. And then I go back in time. I'm me in a veil, and I'm seven and it's my First Communion, and I'm ten and I'm smiling and rubbing a pony's nose and I'm every little girl I ever was right now, in my vulnerability and innocence.* And he's the man that's stolen the adult out of me. But I can't work it out because it's too quick, and my head's swaying with drink and tears, and I can't explain it; it's grief for something, for everything. I wish I could get back what's been lost. I wish I could believe I'll learn from letting it go. I wish I could begin everything again.

All I can say is, 'this is shit.'

I push his hand away, get up, walk.

He doesn't follow.

Declan has been waiting on the edge of the drama with the drinks.

'YOU OK?' he asks. His natural loudness has a normalcy here; everyone is shouting to be heard around us. I don't bother trying to answer. I just nod, gulping down vodka and Red Bull.

'Hey, STEADY MARY,' he advises. Too late, I've finished it off.

'I need the bathroom,' I shout.

'I'm NOT SURPRISED,' he comments, taking my glass.

As I start the push through to the loo, there's Monica, fresh in the door. Surveying the room for ... I see her see R. Her eyes light up and she's instantly moving across to him, shouldering her way through the packed bodies. There's a big grin on her face. Well, what for Monica is a big grin, more like the smirk of the postulant who's just been told she's come tops in the National Nun Exam. She's delighted with herself, in her very own self-contained Monica way.

'Monica?' I call across to her.

Sharply, she turns. Pinched lips – guilt, defense, oh many a thing playing across her eyes.

My head hasn't yet caught up with my mouth. What do I want to say? I want to be crushing, emotional, precise. What's the worse thing I can think of:

'He's starting pre-op next week, be there for him, girlfriend. Sometimes it's hard becoming a woman.'

Or

'I won't bother you guys again until I have the baby.'

Or, or, or…

What I say is, 'All yours, but just so you know – Rory hates fanny shamrocks.' Yes, crude and stupid, bordering on the infantile, but it's the best I can come up with right now. I turn away before her face reacts.

Boy, do I ever need the sanctuary of The Ladies. I have to

queue for a cubicle, the usual malarkey – two per thousand bladders. I rummage in my bag to hide the shame of being near to tears. I'm making a habit of this today. I should suggest to Monica that she create a handbag for Owen de Maguire that's designed to fit discreetly over the head of the crushed woman: Life getting you down? Period due? Pregnant? Kiddies running amuck? Or are you simply involved with a big selfish wanker who you've finally realised doesn't give a flying feck about you? Well, you might need to cry! And cry right now! And now you can! With the new Owen de Maguire *Bag On Yer Head*. This handy handbag slash *bag on your head* fits snuggly over your head, hiding the embarrassment of those hideous tears. Special absorbent lining ensures no embarrassing leaks. And special soundproofing covers the embarrassment of those uncontrollable sobs. Now you CAN be a typical soppy emotional female drip, any time, anywhere you want.

I'm top of the queue and a cubicle opens. Just my luck, it's Clodagh from this afternoon. I'm hoping she won't recognise me.

'Mary McNice, how McNice to see you.' She's in a good mood. 'Are you OK?' she asks.

'Oh grand, you know,' I stutter.

'Come here,' she says. And before I know what's happened, she has dragged me into the cubicle she just vacated.

'Here, I've hardly any left, might as well finish it. And you look like you need it more than I do.' She's unwrapping a few microbes of coke and has mashed me out an infinitesimal line on the toilet top. 'Never buy it, never refuse it' – Cormac's hand-me-down wisdom.

'OK.'

She hands me a sawn-off straw.

'Wow, I'm impressed, so organised. You're definitely producer material, I'll say that,' I say as I squash a nostril and snort the cocaine tracing. There must be pounds of the stuff floating around out there on a dirty night in Dublin, and here ...

'Sorry it's so little,' she reads my mind.

'As the atomic scientist said to the nihilist, it's better than nothing,' I try to amuse us both and manage to make no sense at the same time.

She dabs the remnants from the wrap. I end up having the last lick. Wait. No numbing, no brightening buzz, just a dull fizz. What is this stuff, really? Speed cut with sherbet? Flour? Dandruff? 'Omo,' Cormac calls Dublin coke. Flavio tells me that Cormac is known as 'The Hoover' in Amsterdam, so I presume he knows what he's on about.

'Feck, I really feel my age just this minute, do you ever get that?' I say to Clodagh when we're done. (As if that was why I was near to tears a moment ago? Help! Help! I've been mugged by Time.)

'For sure.'

'What age are you?'

'Twenty-three.'

'I've got to pee,' I tell her.

'Oh, right, right,' she says as she makes to leave, 'you were great on the show today, by the way.'

'Was I?' I ask.

'Yes.'

'Thanks for everything, for the ... stuff.'

'Sure.'

I am Rodin's *Thinker*, drunk on the toilet. Again. OK. Resolve. Resolve. Revolving head, it feels like. Think. Next. Thing. Paddy Finn, Interview, still to write up, now or in the morning? Now?

Now. OK. Plan. Good. Go home. Now. Sense. It makes. Total.

'Hello. Is there, like, anyone in there? I, like, *really* need to use the can.'

This is accompanied by loud knocking. The voice – erghhhhhhh. I exit quickly, irritated.

'What's with the, *LIKE,* American accent?' I berate the bimbo who was knocking.

'Because I'm, *like,* American,' she says, pushing past me and banging the toilet door in her wake.

'Good answer,' I call out, tottering off.

Whatever that shite I snorted was, it hasn't woken up my mind. It's just left me with an aching nostril and a super-glued jaw. I want to go immediately, go, write my piece, e-mail it off, sleep for the weekend, get up bright and early on Monday morning and wonder what the hell it is I'm going to do with the rest of my life.

First the hassle of getting out of here: the unwanted contact, the press of bodies and faces you must acknowledge and nod to, a tap on the shoulder to congratulate you, drink splashes on your arm, the riddle of passing conversation – 'petrodollars v. petroeuros, that's what it's all about,' '$15 in Macys, no way' 'your arse is' ... You plough on, thinking, 'the door, the door' and when you're nearly there, you see Declan and you know you're both going nowhere for a while.

He has cornered Crispin at the end of the bar. Voices are raised.

'No way, man. NO WAY. You're wrong, they're wrong,' Declan is booming. He only uses 'man' as an address when he is mad.

Clearly it is my responsibility to end this now:

'Excuse me, Declan, I have to go, now, please,' I interrupt, standing on Crispin's foot by accident, on purpose, to make my point.

'Wait one minute. Not now,' Declan says to me.

'You *let* it go, man, so do that: LET IT GO,' Crispin has picked up Declan's tone. They're both drunk, Declan more so.

'Well fuck you, you ARSEHOLE,' he says.

'Declan, please,' I attempt, trying to pull him gently away. He violently shrugs my hand off his arm. It hurt. He doesn't notice.

'I've already had that in writing from you today, remember? You're repeating yourself,' Crispin sneers, 'and I think that clarifies not just mine, but the company's and the client's angle on this, so–'

I think he's about to say something along the lines of goodbye, good riddance and up yours, matey. He's certainly turning to terminate the 'conversation', when the scene switches to slowmo. The arch of Declan's punch almost makes contact with Crispin, but he moves just in time and slips free of the impact. Declan's fist lands squarely in a hostess's tray of drinks. Then everything speeds up again: drinks fly off the silver, people jump aside to avoid being drenched, glass smashes on the floor. A glamour puss in a backless top gets the ice-cubes and wet of a long one down the spine. She's squealing with shock and indignation, and her male companion is looking for someone to deck in her defence.

Crispin faces Declan, and in that crucial second when it's about to be ding ding, round one, arrogant Anglo-Irish ad. exec. versus Celtic poet-at-heart senior copywriter, the mad bulls from the door are in. Declan is identified as the culprit, restrained, dragged to the door and manhandled down the stairs before you can say 'hello, chaps. Can we call this quits and just shake on it like gentlemen?'

Crispin's shock is tempered by clear delight that Declan has been taken care of. The wet girl is doing her 'I'm all wet' thing while her handsome man is enjoying dabbing bunched napkins right down to the crack of her arse, and the gapers are shook out of their alco-haze by the sudden flare-up of physical violence. Delighted, reminded they're in real life, not a film. Real life is better, even if it pays less. That's my *amazing* insight as I turn, with difficulty, on my pointy heels, and ...

And there's Rory.

'Are you all right?' he asks.

'No,' I say, pushing past him and lurching down the stairs, away from my ex, The Betrayer, after my friend, The Lunatic.

Declan is outside the door, standing with difficulty, concentrating – as if he's listening to a distant headmaster asking, *Twomey, Declan, present?* And he's not sure of the answer. He's watched by a chorus-line of spread-eagled bouncers. They're blocking the door.

I quickly collect our coats from the coat check and wobble out. I hand Declan his and we walk a little away from the door to regroup. I dust him down, as if in the action I'm wiping the memory of his being roughed out of the club.

He tells me 'thanks.'

'Mm, mm,' I say.

I wave down a taxi, and take pains to convince the driver that we're not a pair of vomitty ne'er do wells. He's chilled; a young fella, well young for a taxi driver. He raises a cool blue eye, smiles and nods for us to get in.

As we pull off, I notice Kian O'Kelly stumbling drunkenly down the street toward The Madra Rua. Just as we're rounding the corner, he trips and falls off the pavement. He's probably news-hounding it down there. All of us are in the gutter, but some of us really are in the gutter.

CHAPTER 17

'**GO** *AND GET IT* – a travesty. A TRAVESTY. **COME** AND GET IT. Listen, listen, I'll say it again. SHUT UP AND LISTEN Mary. COME AND GET IT. What do you hear? What DO you hear?'

'The name you came up with, and yes, it is the best. *Go and Get It* stinks.'

'Yes, yes, true, and no, what you HEAR is the chocolate TALKING to YOU. That's what you hear. See?'

'Yeah,' I say, best to agree.

'And GO. When I say "GO" to you, what's going on there?'

'Crap, it's crap.'

'CRAP, yes. Another voice, who? WHOSE VOICE? Saying GO, GO AND GET IT, but why? WHO? WHY? It's not just YOU and THE CHOCOLATE anymore. Gettit? I rest my case.'

Declan is explaining the to-do with Crispin. *Apparently* the client loves the whole campaign, blah blah blah, but *Come* has to go, it's now *Go*. And they all agree, and Declan has no say because he waved bye-bye. But he thinks the idea is a TRAVESTY. 'A *prima facie* trampling, TRAMPLING ON ME AND MY IDEA.'

I inquire as to why he may care.

'The Last Campaign, the end of the legend. I don't want to exit on the mediocrity of GO, I want the high of COME.'

We're silent as we let that sentiment wash over us.

And this is The Third World Avenger? I think to myself.

'Or why not just something like Mars, that's what I don't get,' the taxi man butts in, friendly enough, I suppose, given that he's just spent the night trolleying home the end-of-week paralytic. And lucid too. Why not, indeed – why not Mars, Pars, Sars or just some feckin' Choccy Bars?

Declan glowers; he's in no mood to laugh this off, yet. I just want to be alone. Thankfully, we've reached my stop. I ask him to pull over. Declan turns to me, his head nodding unsteadily on his shoulders.

'I suppose a ride is out of the question?' he slurs.

'No,' I say.

'No, it's not?'

'No. No as in I am saying "no" to you. We are friends, Deco. Right. Man?'

'But I'm sad. I'm lonely.' He slumps toward me. I shift aside to avoid him and he ends up prone on the back seat. He doesn't get up. I leave him be.

'Here, if you don't mind booting him out when he gets home,' I tell the taxi driver, handing him enough fare for both of us, plus a tip that I hope will mean he won't say no. He doesn't. I give him Declan's address and do my best to hurry out before he can change his mind.

I hear something like a gentle snore from Declan. I ruffle his hair as a good night before I get out. I hope he gets home safe.

OoOoO

I'm sitting in front of my laptop in my pyjamas, tapping my panda-bear slippered foot on the floor. I'm waiting for the computer to boot up. I've left the light low, so the main illumination is from the brightening screen. At this stage all I want to do is get this done – quick. Maybe that's the best way, the way to access the whiz within.

'I didn't know you had it in you,' Miriam will say.

'Neither did I,' I'll laugh. She'll laugh. We'll all be laughing.

I reach out and press rewind on the cassette recorder. The blank page awaits. I press play. A male voice I don't immediately recognise comes out:

' ... with Sun-Saturn and Jupiter rising ... ' I fast forward. '... Dordogne region of France. Have you ever been there? No. Well, ideally that's where you should be living. Ireland's not that good for you, according to the chart, see here ...' Fast forward again. ' ... or Shanghai. Namibia is good ...' ' and Pluto was there throughout that time ... ' and 'Saturn in that angle will ...' and 'Venus is opposing ...' and ' ... not a good year' and 'the future ...' and 'that'll be €100, please'. 'Yes, cash is great'.

No, no, no! I'm listening to my recent session with an astrologer. Much as he was good at listing all my major 'coulds' and 'shoulds', he wasn't strong on immediate dos – like *do* check the tape in the machine before your all-important upcoming interview with Paddy Finn. The Star Gazer was too busy telling me to run away to another country. Maybe the two things are related? Hang on, what's this? '... will a scone do' and 'something spongy with cream and icing' and, 'big chest', and 'kind of gal I am' and 'because I do'. It's the interview. I am saved. *Click*. No. Feck. It's finished. And so am I.

I rummage back through my skimpy notes: *Mad hair – hates interviews, (buns on Miriam?) show about? FUNNY. Ireland – good – home. Older. Novel/screenplay/sitcom. 'Bottom Gear' Darren = Nice. Zack W., racist paedo – N.B. excellent buns, come again …* The only thing my notes tell me is that I should learn shorthand – priority.

I was relying on that tape. But no worries; now it's a case of just surf, and turf a load of internet quotes into a document and string them together into something. My brief was to do it with 'Attitude' anyway, and that's my 'Attitude' – cut and paste. I'll hammer something together, I'll get this done, I'll stay awake…

0o0o0

What time is it? Noise, from where? Ouch. I wake with a crick in my neck; I must have fallen asleep on the sofa. I know I finished the article – the effort of making sense, the effort of playing 'spot the typo' half-sozzled, thinking 'this is mighty' one minute and 'pure shite' the next, and did I send it? Is it sent? Can't recall and it's not that that has awoken me. It's the aggro in the hall outside my front door: raised voices, the banging of doors, a struggle … Must go see.

I watch the drama through my front door peephole, the distorted view makes me think *Arnolfini Wedding Portrait*, but it's the opposite of conjugal bliss through the concave looking glass. There's my lovely O'Sport neighbours, arguing, arguing, arguing. Two miniaturised people curved into dissent in front of me. Oh, *come on*, boys and girls, I think. I know, it would be an excellent idea if I go and tell them 'no, don't do that'. What the world needs now is love, sweet love, and I should know because I haven't a shred of it, in the biblical sense. I have loved and lost and I should tell them how it feels ... I open the door.

As I do, the lift is pinging shut and Ms O'S has gone.

'Piss off, then,' Mr O'S bids her adieu.

I turn and we stare at each for longer than would be polite in the normal course of events, but it's late and it's the weekend and there's been drink and argument all round. What I take in as I look, is: young, good-looking, pissed off, pissed, no top, skin, jeans, fit, mmmmmm. What he must see in me is space-rocket-motif pyjamas, panda-feet slippers, flushed just-awake face, thin line between being a bit drunk/barmy. Maybe, maybe, who knows? You can never *really* know what the other human person is thinking; it's all conjecture from behind the bars of yourself. We're all so different at the end of the day, so different. I'm still half asleep ...

'Well, hello,' he slurs.

'Hello. Are you OK? I heard ...' I manage to say.

'It's nada, believe me.'

'Right so, goodnight,' I say, closing the door.

'Oi, where are you going? I've got drink. How about a chat? I'm lonely. Huh?'

'Ermm,' I dither. Lonely. Where did I hear that before, tonight?

'Come on,' he's insisting, and then I'm saying yes and grabbing my keys and going next door in pyjamas and joke slippers. And it's funny, finally going through the portal to the world of the O'Sports. I half expect them to have a strip of beach in there, with a section of sea foaming away and a couple of deck chairs and a tank with a mini-shark in it, maybe. But no, it's the same cramp as my own, except more so, because there's two of them in it and

they've all the flippers and snorkels and wet suits and goggles and stuff hanging everywhere. You name it, I can't; I'm not into water sports. Although, mental note to self: don't say to O'Sport that you're "not into water sports" *now*, he might take as some sort of twisted come-on. See, I'm not that far out of it that I don't know that here's trouble, maybe.

'Sit yourself down, and will you take a tinny in the hand?' he flourishes at me. He's fairly good craic when he's had a few; he's awful serious if you ever meet him in the morning.

'Whatever you're having yourself, kind sir,' I tell him.

Soon both of us are sitting on the couch, drinking Royal Dutch as nature intended – straight from the can.

I somehow manage to suppress the wave of nausea I feel at each gulp. I'm trying to be a good sport – because Life Must March On, as *The Book of Nuggets* might put it. Feck, forgot to give it to Declan after all. I want to match O'Sport's mood. He's up for a laugh. And he's looking good.

'Should I put on some music?' he asks, and he's getting up.

'Ah, yeah,' I agree.

'What?' he asks as he's reading CD covers. 'James Blunt? Oh puke, can't handle mushy squaddies this time of night. Anything you fancy?'

I can't think, so I tell him, 'you decide.'

'Oh here,' he says, finding something, 'I'll stick this on.'

'What is it?'

'The Best of the Best of Everything,' he says.

'Should be all right,' I laugh.

I try to make polite conversation by asking about watery things, like – 'Do you like this lager? And do you think fish have feelings? And have you ever punched a shark? And what's the worse thing that ever happened to you on a body board?'

At some point he corrects me and tells me, 'flippers' aren't 'flippers'; they're 'fins'. I find that absolutely fascinating and I say, 'well you learn something new every day.' Fins, fins, fins, fins, I repeat to myself, just so I'll remember.

Today is gonna be the day comes on. 'What do you think of his voice?' I ask O'Sport. As the song says, maybe he's going to be the one that saves me. 'Dirty,' he answers.

O'Sport's name is Tiernan, by the way. The girlfriend is Saoirse. He just told me that a minute ago. Anyway, it's all big songs, you know? We're sitting here being literally swept away by the music. All big stuff, like, *I still haven't found what I'm looking for.* 'There's the theme tune to my life,' I laugh when that comes on, and Tiernan is saying at exactly the same time, 'still, I'll have a go at finding it'. And he gets up, goes to the fridge and comes back with what he tells me is the last Royal Dutch. And there I was a minute ago thinking I could barely survive a gulp, and now I'm sharing a third with 'T', that's what I call him now.

Saoirse has gone to her mammy's, T. tells me. I hope she doesn't come back, I think, as he pats me on the shoulder, which becomes his hand on my neck, which makes my head fall toward his bare chest. I'm thinking *body board – body like a board* and let's be frank, we're both lost then in the out of body eroticism of alcohol-fuelled attraction.

I don't know what drives his kiss, but I'm kissing him with all the loss of something I never had. I'm loosened for now and running with the freedom of it. I'm not thinking about *his* girlfriend, not even particularly thinking about *him* per se, as my hands mirror his in exploring the body. He's hard and soft all over and so am I, and eventually then we've enough in common for him to crack open the last of the drink – a bottle of Cab. Sav. – get two glasses and I follow the clink of them to the bedroom. Their bedroom.

The CD is on a loop and Robbie Williams is singing *Through it all* … and that's what's going through my mind. *Through it all, through it all,* we – me and T – have hardly anything to say to each other. And it doesn't matter. We both flow with the flow, we're equally mad into it, we're probably not even experiencing anyways near the same thing. It's just some subsets of ourselves that have crossed for now and we're going with it. But there's nothing to say because the real 'each' of us is safe, tight, silently locked away. Back of the head. Protected. Neither of us is really here at all – I was pissed last night/ I was off me head/ I was gone. All the safety valves are there. I abandon myself completely.

OoOoO

I wake with a splitting headache. It takes a long moment to peel my eyes open. What's happened to my walls? They've changed colour in the night. And my curtains? My curtains have become blinds, and my bed? My bed is the wrong way round and the wrong bed. And my teddy? My teddy's not my teddy; he's a man, and the man is Tiernan, T. - The Next Door Neighbour, I know his name. Nobody knows the name of their neighbours in a Dublin apartment complex. It's Against Nature! Oh God. All I know is that I have to be out of here quicker than a minute ago.

I slip naked from the bed and crawl around the floor, dressing in the few strewn bits that belong to me. On all fours, I exit from the bedroom, landing my knee on a stray flipper, sorry, fin, on the way, but still managing to gather big slippers and get keys. Moving as I rise, like evolving man himself, I come to full-standing at the door.

I take a deep breath. Please, I swear on *The Book of Nuggets,* I'll be good ever after if only, please, let not the girlfriend be just coming up the lift as I–

Run quickly to my front door, struggle in my hurry to stick the key in the door and open up and go in.

I am home. Safe! I fleetingly find it fascinating that I have absolutely no conscience in this matter. Got away with it.

I feel quite nice actually, as I collapse on the bed.

Totally relaxed.

Body happy.

Blackout.

CHAPTER 18

The ringing of the phone wakes me. I let it ring out. What time is it? In answer to my question, the bells of St Patrick's start bashing, and I count out the time. 1,2,3,4,5 … 12. Mid-day. What day? Saturday? What's significant about today? Article. Deadline. Dead. Line. Am. I. Dead?

I rush to the living room. There on the table is my laptop, hibernating. I push the button. I wait for it to wake up. I have no memory of what I wrote, what I did or didn't send last night. I find the document, open it and read:

Paddy Balls/ Suck my Attitude, Miriam...
RE-TITLE BEFORE SEND!!!!!!
Paddy Finn has been described as 'funny', (The Sligo Paper) 'very funny' (The Belfast Paper), 'screamingly hilarious' (The London Paper), 'the funniest thing I have ever seen' (The Melbourne Paper) 'gut-bustingly funny' (The Auckland Paper) 'the best' (The Manchester Paper) 'a genius' (The New York Paper)

'a legend in the making' (The Los Angeles Paper) and 'over--rated, under-talented and laugh-free' (Kian O'Kelly, Dublin Evening News). It will come as no surprise then that he is regarded as Ireland's most successful young comic. He is back in Ireland for a run in Dublin's Curate's Lane. I met up with him in the tea lounge of Dublin's Westbury Hotel.

I arrive late for our interview, having just crawled through a hedge in RTE (don't ask – won't tell). He's easily recognisable – the only pre-menopausal person in the room. He cuts a petulant, adolescent figure, sprawled as he is across a comfy chair. His casual wear and his hair, which squats on his head like a greasy parasite, underline this impression, and it seems confirmed when, having accepted my apologies, he informs me he doesn't like doing interviews. I assuage his antipathy by ordering afternoon tea (ASK MIRIAM CAN PUT THIS ON TAB???) and asking him what we can expect of his show. He's aiming for it be 'funny' I am assured. Old and new material will feature in the show, and we can look forward to an Irish slant from this 'leprechaun love child of Beckett and Lenny Bruce' (The English Paper) 'His show is a peculiarly Irish confection, a slice of shamrock ripple between two world weary wafers' (The Edinburgh Paper). 'perfect, stunning, brilliant and indelibly Irish' (The Chicago Paper), 'Get him off', (Kian O'Kelly, Dublin Evening News).

In addition to the touring, Paddy is busy with writing commissions and has just finished filming Bottom Gear (Scarface set in Cabra, according to the film's pre-release web publicity) alongside Irish über star Darren O'Marra. Paddy says Darren was 'cool' and 'a good bloke to work with' when they shot their thirty-second scene together.

Paddy is reluctant to analyse his own work. He has said in the past, 'talking about comedy is like trying to personalise frog spawn'. He admits to admiring the work of the late US stand-up Zack Whammy, he of the famous catchphrase, 'I've got problems, what's your excuse', but says he has never looked to outside himself for a blueprint when it comes to creating material. The 29-year-old's current show is called 'Older', a reference to a decade of experience successfully plying his comedic trade: 'total sell-out success' (The Sydney Paper), 'had the capacity audience in the palm of his hand' (The Hong Kong Paper) 'tickets like gold dust' (The San Francisco Paper) '3000 audience members were on their feet in sustained ovation at the end' (The Montreal Paper) 'what a bag of shite' (Kian O'Kelly, Dublin Evening News).

Paddy is vague about the reasons he got involved in comedy. 'That's the bus I got on,' he tells me. He is famously regarded as 'sexy': 'ninety minutes of glorious Irish hunk' (The Adelaide Ladies Paper), 'creamy delivery from comedy dream boy' (The Boston Ladies Paper), 'give me the chance to not throw him out of bed for eating biscuits' (The Newcastle Ladies Paper), 'unfunny bog trotter, sounds like slurry, smells like boring' (Kian O'Kelly, Dublin Evening News), but it's not something he claims to be aware of himself. He is a married man and expecting his first child shortly, he tells me, as if that completely explains away the issue. 'Paddy ur a ride u big boyo' is the coyest of a hundred such messages posted on his official website.

Wife and child, or no wife and child, you can imagine he needs to carry a big anti-groupie stick at all times to beat off the doting lady fans. He asks me if am I married myself, and do I have children. The answer is absolutely 'no and no', despite the fact, I tell him, that I inadvertently suggested I was engaged on television earlier in the day. In fact I tell him the whole long-winded story, and he proves a good listener. (Did he have any other choice, I reflect now, later. Too late!) Anyhow, while we're on the subject of me, imagine my surprise a few hours later when I discovered my 'boyfriend' of three and a half years has been shagging one of my 'best' friend. Thank you, Rory Trevelyan. Thank you, Monica Duffy. Toward the end of our interview, Paddy explains to me why he is a reluctant interviewee. In the past he's been attributed with quotes he never made, most infamously the tsunami 'let them eat cake' headline. Far from the petulance I'd initially assumed, he says his only concern is the 'authenticity' of his live work – that it should have the ring of truth. He refers to himself as a 'Truth Trader'. Interviews such as this one are, as he sees it, necessary evils. Having expounded at length on this point, he leaves me, saying that he'll just have to trust I won't 'stitch him up'. He's been left with a suspicion of journalists. I assure him I'm not one, I'm just a columnist. He asks what the difference is and I answer 'laziness probably'. At which he laughs.

No, hang on, now that I recall, he didn't laugh. He said, 'very funny'. Which I take to be the professional laughter-merchant's equivalent of a laugh. And with that, he mooches off into the ether, on his quest for truth.

'Love many, trust few,' my father always said, though it was Shakespeare who said it first. Was he right? Read the above and answers on a postcard please.

Please God, I didn't send this article, this rambling, quote-ladened, over-personalised excuse for an interview. Its only saving grace being that I obviously ran it though the spellcheck.

But to conclude on a muse about love and trust? What am I, a nun now? Is that the Julie Andrews effect that booze, crap drugs and being cheated on has on me – is that the Von Trapp I've fallen into? I wish I could laugh but I can't – I know in my heart and soul this is exactly the kind of thing that Miriam absolutely *hates*.

Into *Outlook Express,* I click on *Sent Items* and, heart sinking, I read:

—— Original Message ——
From: Mary McNice
To: miriam@theirelander.ie
Subject: Read this!
Attached: Paddy Finn Suck my Attitude Miriam
Hi Miriam

It's bloody late/early but here it is!! I am aware of ur negative feelings toward 'Attitude' of recents. Well as you suggest here's a stub at some a bit different – interview and attitude in one. Hey what about 'Is it?' What do you think of that as a new title insteud of 'Atittude' – me interview a different person every week like this? You wanna shake it up a bit. Ne pas?

Have a thing.

Let me now.

Dead to hear what ur think!

Excues me now, off to bed, knackered – read attached!!!!!!

Mary X X

It was sent. It is gone. Oh God! The typos, look at all the feckin' typos! The delighted-with-itself email lashed off in passion and not even re-read before being sent. Miriam, I never use spellcheck in my e-mails, is that an excuse? It was late, I was drunk, upset, emotional, wrecked from the effort of trying to make sense in the article and momentarily insane. Will any of those do as an excuse? Am I covered, Miriam? No, I know, no! And what about the tone – Miriam is nothing if not formal. She'd have everyone addressing her as Your Excellency, The Midweek Editor, if she could get away with it. And I actually wrote 'knackered' in an e-mail to Miriam? 'The Queen's English only here,' she's always saying. She takes that sentiment as if it were her personal family honour.

And the exclamation marks! 'Leave the childish punctuation to Enid Blyton' – another classic Miriamism. *And then*, signing off with an 'x x'? To Miriam? Kiss, kiss to hard-news, hard-nosed, hard-as-nails-but-a-lot-harder Miriam. Miriam *the* journalist – by definition a heart of brick and a brain with the very synapses built of cynicism?

Jesus, has she got it yet, what did she say? I can fairly well predict ...

There are three e-mails in the InBox.

One -
—— Original Message ——
FROM: Miriam Cromwell
TO: mmcnice@eircom.net
SUBJECT: Paddy Finn
ATTACHED: Paddy Finn Press Release – Curate's Lane
Hello Mary

Please find attached the press release for interview as promised.

Remember the details? Westbury Hotel, 4pm. You know what he looks like, I'm sure. If not, may I suggest googling a photograph.

If it could be with me tomorrow morning, that would be great.
MC

Two -

—— Original Message ——

From: Miriam Cromwell

To: mmcnice@eircom.net

Subject: FW: Legal action.

Mary,

Perhaps you can enlighten us to as to what the below is all about?

I do not take the threat of legal action lightly, and neither will the Managing Editor.

Given that such threat has been made, I would like a written explanation from you asap.

And allow me confirm: I never requested, sanctioned or suggested the use of trespass, theft or any infringement of commonly held legal bounds in the fulfilment of your contractual obligations to this paper.

As far as I am concerned you were <u>not</u> acting on behalf of the paper, and I am appalled that you have brought such suspicion upon Midweek and I. I requested you be at the Westbury Hotel at 4pm this afternoon, to interview Paddy Finn. It appears you were distracted with other business.

Explanation please?

M

—— Original Message ——

From: Attracta Butt

To: mcromwell@theirelander.ie

Subject: FW: Legal action.

Dear Miriam

Earlier this afternoon I returned to my office to find Mary

McNice, author of your 'Attitude' column, hiding under my desk. It appears that she was snooping for an inside scoop on plans for this season's Pratt's Late Jape (my project as you know) – this in the context of TV3's planned assault on our ratings. You may or may not be aware that she has a personal connection to the proposed host of their new show? Does she intend using her column to get digs in on behalf of Dugsy? She managed to run away before security could apprehend her and search her person and possessions for any material she may have lifted. The fact that she literally RAN more than confirms my suspicions.

At this juncture we have been unable to assess what, if anything, she did get away with, but my researchers' desks were unattended at the time, as were stacks of notes, schedules and ideas for future items. (She knows her way around this place, Miriam – she knew what she was looking for.) I have big and ground breaking ideas for the show, Miriam, precious ideas, special ideas – confidential ideas, and I want to keep them that way. I felt I should contact you personally first rather than go straight ahead and bring in the Garda Síochána.

Miriam, I feel personally violated and I'm sorry to have to put this in writing to you of all people, but:

If ANY mention of Brian Pratt, me or my programme appears in that person's column I will have no option but to consider legal action. I have already discussed this with the legal department and they are fully behind me on this. We are appalled and disgusted at her behaviour. She obviously feels she has scores to settle, and be warned, unbeknownst to you it appears she plans to use your Wednesday Supplement to do so. Shocking isn't it? I find it shocking. I'm still in shock as I write this, my hands are shaking as I type …

(I'll see you at Quinlivan's dinner party tonight; let's keep this messy business out of that.)
Kindest regards
Attracta

Oh. Pass the Pouilly Fumé, they're chums. They would be. That's Dublin. Everything becomes clear.

Three -
———— Original Message ————
From: Miriam Cromwell
To: mmcnice@eircom.net
Subject:
Ms McNice,

 Your commission arrangements with Midweek are cancelled forthwith.

 Your 'interview' is testament to the fact you cannot keep within a brief, and it, and the efforts I have had to make on your behalf to stave off any legal repercussion from the national broadcaster, are merely the final straw. Your contributions over the four months since I took over as editor have been consistently below par and, frankly, a disappointment.

 I feel there is no further discussion to be had on the matter.
MC

And I'm out. Just like that. What can I say, is there anything I can do? Phone up Miriam, e-mail Attracta, ask them if we can't all get together and sort this out over a chicken? Or better still, go the whole hog, have both of them, *and* their media-other-things husbands over, throw a painter-poet-historian into the mix, and a few actor/writers about to publish their 'new bestsellers' and a couple of academic/politico/gadabouts and maybe even a celebrity priest. Make a right royal dinner party of it. I'll check with you beforehand, Miriam, just to make sure they're *all* UP not DOWN. And I guarantee, this will be well beyond chicken – how about mongoose with a heather and loganberry jus, followed by yam and chilli ice-cream? That sound good? Sound NOW or THEN, Miriam? What is NOW, right now? I don't know. You know, Miriam, you're the one who makes it up.

Am I finished now?

CHAPTER 19

There's another e-mail in my in-box, from the dating website. 'Sakiman' has sent me a message. Seeing as I don't have anything else in particular to do, ever again, I click onto the site and read his message.

> You look nice lady, nice red hair, like flame on head. You like come up and see me sometime! E-mail return please, look forward.

See, Miriam, see? Some people value me. Some people would like to marry me. Some people who don't even know me. I click on his profile:

> Sakiman own own business, like travel, travel lot, like lady, like spend money on lady and all good thing in life. He also like sport car.

His picture shows what looks like a sumo wrestler sitting on the bonnet of what looks like a Porsche – a red one. Red's a positive colour, isn't it? And Porsches cost a packet, don't they? I'm just looking for signs.

He lives in Toyko, **in place big for two**.

Well, if he's looking at two of him, it must be big. Boy, does he sound tempting.

Japanese can't be that hard to learn, can it? And the writing looks so lovely it'd be worth it. Me sitting there in my kimono in our Zen garden, under our tree, painting letters to his family. Me at 5am in the Tokyo fish market:

'Ah, you don't fool me just 'cause me Irish,' I laugh to the man, in fluent, accent-perfect Japanese. Me running home in my wooden shoes, to chop and serve – just like that – no cooking involved!

Or maybe we can afford servants – two ladies in white face paint and pristine little socks scrubbing the kitchen and checking to see if I'd like another cup of gunpowder. Yes, please, just leave it here beside the Mahjong board.

Oh, sorry, that's Chinese isn't it? Don't muddle your cultures, nothing make Sakiman madder. Sorry, Sakiman.

Me wandering around all day like Scarlett Johansson in *Lost in Translation*, only bigger. But that's OK. I'm pregnant. I've got a shopping bag full of writhing eels for Sakiman's tea. I'm over-awed by the sheer neon of everything and quietly looking forward to battering the heads of the fishy fellas with the special Japanese eel-head hammer when I get home. Oh, the oriental domesticity of it!

And the kids could always come back and spend the summer in Claredunny with Mammy. Learn the *cúpla focal* and foot some turf. Oriental babies are so cute. We'd have one of each, a Mary-Machika and a Fumitake-Pat.

They'd sit at the kitchen table in Claredunny, making origami cows and donkeys, while Mam asks, 'you like sausage? You like rasher with sausage? Sausage, rasher sandwich, yum yum. You like God, you like Catholic God? He best in world ever.'

Reality hits. I delete the message.

I pick up the phone to ring Mammy, to tell her I'm getting the two-thirty train, ask her can I stay the weekend, and the week, and maybe the month and the next, maybe six or a year even, would that be OK, Mammy? The call saver tone on the phone tells me there's a message. I bang in the code. It's Rory.

'Hi, Mary. I hope you got home OK after the incident in the club. Declan seemed pretty far gone to me. We should talk. Call me. Take care, boobie.'

That's all. I listen to it again. Seventeen times. I only stop when I accidentally erase it. But by then every syllable, intonation, pause, breath and stop have been indelibly grooved on my memory. I note that he didn't mention our conversation. He didn't mention Monica. He didn't mention the end of Isobel. He didn't mention that I was crying over him. He didn't mention the words 'cheat', 'liar', 'betrayal' or 'sorry'. But he did call. And he did say 'boobie'. He's still thinking about me, see. The ball's in my court now, even if it's bust.

I'll leave it lying there a while, it's not going anywhere.

I sit looking at the phone. I decide to have a shower. I make a cup of tea. I sit on the sofa. There's no food in the house. I ought to get on with the day. What day? I shuffle around the room …

I'm just about to shut off the computer when I notice a new message in my inbox. What else can this be, Sakiman now electronically stalking me? No, actually. It's something else entirely:

—— Original Message ——
From: Sterling Parker
To: mmcnice@eircom.net
Subject: Offer
Dear Ms. McNice,

Emailing you with proposition – you may consider over the weekend? At dinner party last night, conversation into the small hours – on topic of 'personality' columnists –– Miriam Cromwell reads excerpt of your Paddy Finn interview from her BlackBerry, coincidentally remarking that you are off The Irelander's payroll.

Her loss, my gain, I'm thinking – in short, liked what I heard, certain shambolic veracity, could use something in that vein perhaps. Offering you three-month trial. Call me Tuesday. We'll discuss in detail then. Like your attitude and can make it worth your while.

Sincerely yours
Sterling Parker
Editor, Sunday Today (Irish edition)

I read it again just to make sure I read what I think I read, and again, looking for the clue as to who is taking the mick, and then over and over until finally it starts to sink in that maybe this is true? Incredible as the scenario seems, a picture of it evolves in the re-readings:

It's late, they've all been lashing into the vino, voices are raised and now Miriam is shushing everyone to ram home her side of the argument. She's in the company of people who are always right, but naturally she knows she's the rightest. She produces her pièce de resistance, fresh from her BlackBerry, (is she ever not working?) containing my freshly-minted interview. 'Par exemple,' she declaims, reading out a paragraph or so of my effort, spicing it up with a rendition of my shambolic accompanying e-mail.

'Oh don't, don't. That's not fair,' perhaps one voice pipes. Miriam has already dropped my name as the author. But, amid the ripple of laughter and loose words, the casual clink of late-night glasses and the fog of after-dinner cigars, 'no,' she insists, and she continues. She'd be loath to admit it, but she herself has probably had a dram too many. What exactly is she proving by reading out my article? 'I'm just making a point,' she declares, tapping her glass with her BlackBerry to garner everyone's attention. And her point, when she gets to it, is a jumble summarised by: what a sorry state the universe is in when she has to share it with such shoddy scribblers as me.

But, universe or no universe, she doesn't have to share her Wednesday Supplement with me. *Midweek* is Miriam's baby now, and Mary McNice is history, she tells them. Her declaration gets swept away in the ebb and flow of subsequent chatter, but Sterling Parker's interest has been pricked. And Miriam's uncharacteristic indiscretion becomes my unbelievable opportunity. Is it as simple as that? Yes, it appears so. But it will only seem real when I tell someone.

I have to call someone now, share the news, make it tangible. But who? Monica? No, but of course not. Breege? No, not now. She has a new baby. She'll have time to chat some other time. Fourteen or fifteen years down the road. Rory? Call Rory – hi Rory, it's boobie here ... Don't think so.

Mam. Call Mam? No. Imagine the conversation: *What, a job offer? Just maybe? So not sure? And how much might it pay? You don't know? Did I tell you Dolores Kennedy was down the other weekend in her new BMW? She had a smashing Mr Dolores strapped in the passenger seat and her lovely legal wig on her head. I asked her how was she getting on and she blew her nose in a fifty-euro note in answer –* or words to that effect.

No, Mammy, not yet.

No, the lucky winner has to be – Declan.

He sounds awful.

'Mary, what are calling me at this UNGODLY hour for?'

'It one o'clock in the afternoon.'

'Is it? Oh Jesus. OH MY HEAD. I just woke up. You just woke me up.'

I don't want to tell him immediately, when he's not fully compos mentis, instead I joke:

'Yeah, sorry to bother you, just doing a My Typical Saturday Q and A. Tell me, Declan Twomey, what's a typical Saturday for you?'

'Well,' he says, picking up my theme, 'I generally like to sleep ...'

'And?'

I just get an earful of him breathing.

'Declan?'

'Shh, wait, I'm thinking ...'

The challenge of outdoing himself has pulled him awake. I can just see him lying on his back in his crumpled bed, surrounded by creased paperbacks, probably still wearing last-night's shirt, his hair a rough halo sleep-flattened to the pillow, and the phone mashed to his ear, his eyes searching for inspiration in his peeling ceiling.

'OK, right. Typical Saturday, CHEZ DEC TWOMEY – I usually get up late, and am immediately to be found in the kitchen, making French toast with mulberry compote, my weekend speciality, for fifteen or so close friends, will have that with them and a couple of cafetières on the decking out back, chat about the week just flown, then we'll decamp to The Forty Foot for the weekly dip, an absolute ritual with me and the crew, then it's into town for beers, pizzas, maybe a gig, a film, a club, a banquet-clambake-fiesta-knees-up-jamboree, what have you, you know yourself ...' his fluent drone tapers off.

'Gets a bit vague there toward the end, God is in the details, Declan,' I tell him. It's something he's always telling me.

'I'm KNACKERED. I give up.'

'OK. How about your Typical Saturday is brunch with me in one hour from right now?'

'Sure,' he agrees.

'On me.'

'You don't have to ...'

'Because I just got the most extraordinary e-mail, and I have to tell someone, that's why I'm calling.'

'What, what is it?'

'I have to tell you face to face. I have to see your face when I tell you. I want to see what you really think.'

'Tell me what?' he insists. I know Declan hates this kind of suspense. He's totally awake now.

'I'll tell you in Odessa,' I persist.

'What time did you say again?' he asks.

'In one hour.'

'I'll be there, McMystery.'

'Great.'

'Oh, and I've got something I want to tell you,' he adds, in a tone that suggests he's just remembered.

'What?'

'It's about last night.'

'But I was with you last night,' I remind him.

'Wait and hear,' he says, 'isn't that the new rule?

'OK, enigma man.'

'All right, enigma woman.'

'Odessa.'

'Odessa.'

Our conversation ending like a secret code, we ring off.

We are meeting in South Central Dublin's favourite brunch spot in one hour. I'll ring ahead and book a table. We'll both order eggs benedict when we're there, and Declan will say, 'Bloody Mary' and I'll say, 'Stop insulting me, you fiend,' and he'll say, 'I'll take that as a yes,' and he'll order two, one with extra Tabasco. I know. That's today.

I leap into the shower and am soon in a Celtic Earth lather. The unique cleansing properties of briar and what-have-you scrub away yesterday – from Trashing Pants to T O'Sport next door: all down the plughole in a pile of hedgerow suds.

Soon I'm out the door again, down the lift, in the courtyard. Searching my bag for sunglasses, I find yesterday's engagement ring. Impulsively, I fling it in the air. It sails away from me in a quick silvery arc and lands with a low thump in the caretaker's geraniums. Nope, I've never really been much of a one for the rings.

Out in the street, the trees are bursting tips of green, bird song breaks over traffic boom, an intermittent breeze scuds bits of litter along the grey pavement, and above all snatches of luminous cerulean show through breaking cloud.

I throw an eye up the length of St Patrick's spire and a sudden kiss of sunshine lights the newly gilded cross at the top. In that brief blaze it seems some divine sky-energy is conducted down, in a torrential flash, hitting the earth in a flare of radiant roots, splaying out, bedding the celestial in this ground, and with it blessing all those who pass here with the gift of gratitude – for this place – for this new day – for the pulse of things.

And I think to myself, I'm still drunk.

FOR MORE GREAT BOOKS CHECK OUT